G000065356

SEAR

For

Faith

by

KRISTEN MIDDLETON

Dedicated to my insightful psychic friend, Ruth Lordan, who saw something in my future that I certainly didn't see coming. I truly believe that she has an amazing gift, and had we never met, I'd still be selling furniture.

http://www.ruthlordan.com/

Other books by author Kristen Middleton

Blur
Shiver
Vengeance
Illusions

Venom
Slade
Toxic
Claimed by the Lycan

Jezebel
Deviant

Enchanted Secrets
Enchanted Objects
Enchanted Spells

Origins
Running Wild
Dead Endz
Road Kill
End Zone

Planet Z

Romance under pen name K.L. Middleton

Recommended For ages 18 and older due to sexual situations and language.

Tangled Beauty
Tangled Mess
Tangled Fury

Sharp Edges

Billionaire at Sea
Billionaire at Sea Book 2

Gritty biker romance under pen name Cassie Alexandra

For ages 18 and older. Vulgar language and sexual content.

Resisting the Biker
Surviving the Biker
Fearing the Biker
Breaking the Biker
Taming the Biker
Loving the Biker

Prologue

Sunday
November 12th
2:52 pm

Moon Lake Park
Duluth, MN

TODAY WAS THE day.

He would finally get his daughter back and nobody would ever come between them again.

Nobody.

Especially not Barbara.

He tightened his grip on the steering wheel. Thinking of his wife made him want to smash something. The cow had thought she was so incredibly smart by sneaking away with Faith in the middle of the night. But he'd finally located his princess and now the joke would be on her. He'd take Faith back and they'd move to Alaska. Barbara would never think to look for them there.

Take that, bitch.

Grinning to himself, he pulled into a parking spot, far from everyone else, and was pleased to see that he'd arrived at the soccer fields just in time. Several youth teams were about to finish up their games and Faith was among the players.

7

Turning off the engine, he put on a Twins baseball cap and checked his reflection in the rearview mirror. With the eyeglasses, gray wig, and fake moustache he'd purchased over the internet, nobody would recognize him. Not that there was anything to worry about – he was an hour away from his own neck-of-the-woods.

Whistling, he climbed out, went around to the back of the van and opened the door. Inside was a white and brown five-month-old Beagle sitting inside her kennel and chewing on a rawhide bone.

"You ready to get out?" he asked, smiling.

She wagged her tail and barked.

"I know you're anxious, Maisie. So am I," he said, leaning forward to unlock the cage. As soon as he pulled the door open, the excited puppy barreled out and began attacking his face with joyful licks.

Laughing and petting her, he managed to hook the leash onto Maisie's collar and lower the puppy to the ground. Immediately, she tried wandering off.

"Sit," he ordered, pulling back gently on the leash.

Maisie sat down and stared up at him.

Leaning back into the van, he grabbed an oak Derby walking cane and then checked his pockets to make sure he was well prepared. Satisfied, he closed the door and looked back down at the dog. "Okay, let's go and get our girl."

Sniffing the ground, the puppy relieved herself in the grass and then tried charging forward, wanting to get closer to the excitement. One thing for certain – Maisie loved children and they loved her. She was a good pup and he knew when his daughter saw her, it would be love at first sight.

Steering the animal toward the playground, which was in front of the soccer fields, the man scanned the perimeter, looking for her. It wasn't easy spotting his daughter, however, as most of the kids looked the same with their soccer gear on. But then... there she was. He grinned.

Faith.

Yes. This child was definitely his; he was certain of it this time. The last girl he'd taken had been a regrettable mistake. Same with the one before that. Unfortunately, he'd been forced to kill the girls to avoid prison. He couldn't take any risks that might land him behind bars. Faith needed him to find her. To rescue her from Barbara. The sneaky, conniving bitch.

His blood boiled once again as he thought about the woman. What he really wanted was to kill *her*. But, it was too risky, especially since he'd be the first suspect. As for the other two little girls he'd been forced to deal with, he blamed Barbara. She should be the one going to prison for stealing Faith from him like a thief in the night and making him hunt for his own child.

"Go, Amy!" hollered one of the coaches.

He looked back toward the far field. Faith's blonde ponytail bounced in the wind as she dribbled the ball toward the other team's net. She missed, by a longshot, but his heart filled with pride at her assertiveness.

"That's my girl," he murmured, watching her charge back toward the ball again. "A chip off of the old block."

Soccer had once been everything to him. He'd played goalie all through high school and into college, until the injuries. First, he'd gotten kicked in the head by another player during a tournament, rendering him unconscious. He woke up in an ambulance and

9

fortunately, there'd been no severe damage to his brain, just some temporary memory loss. That put him out of commission for six weeks. Making matters worse, two weeks after he returned to the field, he blew out his kneecap. Things were never the same, thus ending his dreams of becoming a paid, professional soccer player. It had been quite a blow and for months, he'd wallowed in self-pity, despair, and finally… rage. When he wasn't depressed about his life, he was screaming and hollering at the people around him. He lost a lot of friends and soon, nobody wanted to have anything to do with him. It became so bad that his mother talked him into seeing a therapist and that's when he was diagnosed with *Intermittent Explosive Disorder*, possibly brought on by the injury to his head. He was put on medication, and even he had to admit, the pills seemed to help him get his life back in order. Eventually, he found a job making decent money, moved out of his mother's place, and started online dating. That's when he met Barbara, the love of his life. At least that's what he'd thought… until she'd turned on him and took his daughter away.

He sensed that his anger was starting to get the best of him and realized he'd forgotten to take his medication again. He closed his eyes and counted backward from twenty, trying to imagine things that made him happy. Like reuniting with his daughter. Picturing the wonderful life they'd have together, he smiled and opened his eyes.

See, you don't need them anymore.

Getting Faith back would be better than any medication. Besides, his life wasn't all that bad to begin with and he couldn't wait to share it with her. It was obvious that he and the girl on the field were related – they had so many things in common. Especially soccer, which was perfect, because he was now one of the assistant coaches in the traveling youth squad at the local elementary school. It was how he'd found Faith. Three weeks before, his team had played against theirs and that's when he'd noticed her. Surprisingly, she hadn't recognized him. Neither had her mother, thank goodness.

As he walked with the cane, he glanced back over to the field, where the parents were sitting. None of them looked like his ex, but that didn't mean anything. More than likely she had changed both of their identities and was in disguise. His eyes rested on a heavyset woman with sunglasses and blonde hair pulled back into a ponytail. She was talking to another woman, not even paying attention to the game.

He grunted.

That definitely could be her.

Barbara had no interest in soccer, or any sport. But she always had a passion for food, which would explain the extra pounds.

He squinted.

Yes, the woman did resemble her slightly. He just couldn't be certain. Faith looked the same, however. He'd know the beautiful profile of his daughter anywhere. The problem was – she wouldn't recognize him, which was why he'd brought the chloroform and the puppy. There wouldn't be any resistance, and once she woke up, he'd explain everything. Faith would understand, too. She was just that special.

Anticipating their reunion, he smiled as he sat down at a nearby bench, facing the park. He was taking a gamble that after the game, Faith would rush over and play at the park. He'd watched her do it the last couple of weekends, after taking time off from coaching his school's games, to study her habits.

Claps and cheers from the soccer field erupted and he knew it was almost time to take action. Shortly after, he saw Faith running toward the swings with another girl.

"There she is, Maisie," he murmured, sitting up straighter. "Our princess."

"Oh, Jamie! Look at the puppy!" cried Faith, looking his way.

"He's *so* cute!" gushed the other girl, a short redhead with curly hair and pale, freckled skin.

Hiding a smile, he let go of Maisie's leash and she took off in their direction. The children squealed with delight as the pup raced over to them. Soon, both were petting Maisie and giggling as she licked their hands and barked happily.

He stood up slowly, as if in pain. "Excuse me, girls, could you help me with my dog?" he called, raising his hand in the air. "I have arthritis and my knees are killing me today. I don't want to have to chase her all over the park."

Faith grabbed the leash and they walked Maisie back over to where he was leaning on the cane. "Here you go." She handed him the leash.

"Thank you," he replied, glancing over their heads. There were no parents yet. Only a couple of boys on the monkey-bars and they weren't paying much attention. Still, he had to make a move quickly.

"You're welcome," said Faith.

He rubbed his knee and moaned.

"Are you okay?" asked Jamie, looking concerned.

12

He grinned sadly. She was a cute kid. He didn't want to have to hurt her and hoped it wouldn't come to that. "Just old."

"My grandmother is older than you and she still jogs," said Jamie.

His smile fell. "How nice for her. You want a treat, Maisie?" he asked the dog.

Hearing the signal, she started barking excitedly and he grinned again. He'd been training her for the last few weeks. All he had to do was mention the word "treat", let go of the leash, and she'd run toward the back of the van.

"Her name is Maisie? That's cute," said Faith.

He took a long look at Faith's face. Standing this close to the girl, he thought she looked a little older than seven.

It's her. You're being paranoid, he told himself.

"We should go and play on the swings before our parents come," said the redhead, taking a step back. She looked down at the dog. "Goodbye, Maisie."

"Goodbye," said Faith, bending down to pet the Beagle again.

"Maisie, you want a treat?" he asked firmly, this time, letting go of the leash.

The dog took off, heading straight for the van.

"Oh no," he said, pretending to panic. "Someone needs to catch her before she gets hit by a car."

"I'll go!" cried Faith, taking off after the dog.

"Me, too!" hollered the other girl, chasing after her friend.

He looked toward the fields and noticed that the parents had packed up their lawn chairs and would soon head toward the parking lot. Knowing that there was no more time to lose, he turned around and rushed after the girls. He found them exactly where he knew they'd be – standing behind the van, petting the dog again, and laughing.

"You two young ladies have been such a great help today," he said, opening up the back door while keeping an eye out for witnesses. Thankfully, there was a good distance between the soccer fields and the parking lot. Plus, he'd parked in the very back row, away from the other cars. He just hoped that nobody had noticed the two girls running after the dog. "Can you lift her inside?"

"Sure," said the redhead, picking up Maisie.

He opened up the kennel.

"Okay, let me get her a treat before you release her, or she might run off," he said, moving behind the girl so he could block Faith's view. He tossed a biscuit into the cage. "Now you can let her go."

She did what he told her to do and the dog bolted into the kennel after the treat.

"Great job." He quickly took the chloroformed-infused rag out of his pocket, and before she knew what was happening, covered Jamie's mouth with it. The girl went limp quickly and he let her go. She sunk down to the pavement.

"Oh, my God, what's wrong with Jamie?" cried Faith.

He turned around and gave Faith a wide-eyed stare. "I… I don't know. I think your friend may have fainted. Is she allergic to dogs? We should call an ambulance."

Confused and frightened, Faith's eyes began to fill with tears. "I don't know. Jamie?!" She leaned down and tried shaking the other girl. "Wake up!"

Anxious, the dog began to bark.

14

"Maisie, shush," he said, throwing her another treat.

"She's not waking up," cried Faith.

With her attention still diverted, he quickly reached around Faith's head and put the rag over her mouth.

"I'm so sorry, sweetheart," he murmured into her hair as she tried to struggle. Within seconds, Faith also went limp. He kissed the top of her head.

Damn you, Barbara. This is your fault...

"Jamie! Where are you?" hollered one of the parents.

"Amy!" cried another.

Trying not to panic, he quickly shoved both girls into the van, slammed the door shut, and walked around to the front. As he got in, he avoided eye contact with some of the parents now heading into the lot.

"That was a close one, Maisie," he said, wiping the beads of sweat from his forehead. "Now... what to do with the redhead?"

He thought about killing her, but he knew that Faith would never forgive him. Instead, he decided to take a chance and let Jamie go. She hadn't seen his "real" face, and by the time the police questioned her, the van would have different license plates and be back in Two Harbors. So, he drove to a secluded park near the edge of town, and left the girl on a bench near a jungle gym.

Getting back into the vehicle, he let out a sigh of relief. It was finished. Someone would find the girl or she'd regain consciousness and seek help. Feeling good about what he'd done, he looked over his shoulder. Maisie was lying next to Faith, who was still unconscious. "It's just Maisie, you, and me now, pumpkin. Just like it was meant to be. I'm going to be the best daddy, too. The very best. You just wait and see."

Chapter 1

Gooseberry Falls State Park, MN

Friday, November 17th
3:39 pm

"BACK AGAIN, HUH?"

Startled, Carissa turned away from the falls, and looked at the stranger. He was tall, with jet-black hair, a five-o'clock shadow, and warm, rich brown eyes. Although the man wasn't wearing a badge or uniform, her first impression was that he was either a police officer or park ranger.

"Uh, yeah," she replied, shoving her hands into the pockets of her black wool jacket. She'd been so caught up in her thoughts, that she hadn't noticed how cold it had gotten throughout the course of the day. "I'm sorry, have we met?"

The man stepped closer and smiled. "No. I work for the DNR and just remembered seeing you. My name is Alex. Alex Richardson," he said, holding out his hand.

Carissa quickly looked away, pretending that she didn't see him offer it. Skin-to-skin contact might throw her off-course. She needed to focus on why she was there. "Carissa Jones."

His smile falling, Alex looked down toward the falls. They were standing over the top and the view of the forest below was breathtaking. "It's incredible, huh?"

"Yes. It's beautiful up here. Especially now that the leaves have changed over," she said, stepping out of the way as four hikers moved past them along the path.

"This is definitely my favorite time of the year," he replied. "Although, we're supposed to be getting a winter storm here later."

"I heard," she replied. The forecast had mentioned several inches.

"So, do you live in the area?"

"No. I'm just visiting, up from the cities."

"Whereabouts?"

"I live in Vadnais Heights," she replied.

He leaned against the railing. "I know exactly where that is. I have a friend who lives close by in Shoreview. What brings you out here? Family?"

The man was asking a lot of questions, but she sensed that it was his way. "No. I just needed to come out here."

He stared at her in amusement. "To get away from the hub-bub of the big city?"

Carissa looked down below toward the evergreens, the birch trees, and the winding gorge. "I wish it were that simple. The truth is... I came out here to find someone."

His eyebrows rose. "You did? Who?"

"I'm not exactly sure."

It was a strange answer and even she looked a little perplexed about it.

He chuckled. "Looks like you have your work cut out for you then."

Carissa glanced at him and smiled grimly. "I know. It doesn't make much sense, does it?"

Alex was a pretty good judge of character and something told him that if he kept asking questions, her answers would just get more baffling. But, it was in his nature to pry and this was her second trip out to the falls in two days. Not that it was unusual, but she'd been alone both times and had stood in the same spot for hours, deep in thought. And, the truth was, he was bored as all hell and she was a very attractive woman. With her dark auburn hair and piercing green eyes, Carissa was both stunning and intriguing.

"It must make some sense to you, because you've come all this way in search of this person," Alex replied.

"Do you believe in intuition?"

"I'm a forest ranger and work in law enforcement. I believe that there are times when you need to follow your gut instincts."

Carissa stared at him so hard, it was as if she was looking right into his soul. "That's why you left your wife. You went home, unexpected from work, one day. You knew something wasn't right. You found her in bed with someone else."

Alex stared at her, dumbfounded. "How did you know about that?" He frowned. "Who told you?"

Carissa blinked and her cheeks turned red. "I'm sorry. I didn't mean to blurt that out. It was very insensitive of me."

"Who told you about that?"

"Nobody *told* me. I just get these visions. I'm sorry. I should go," said Carissa, looking embarrassed.

"What, like psychic impressions?"

18

Although Alex had an open mind, he had a hard time believing in the supernatural. That included psychics, mediums, or Ouija boards.

Carissa nodded.

"Did my ex-wife, Patty, put you up to this?" he asked, his eyes narrowing. He could see her trying a stunt like that. She'd been wanting to get back with him and it would be just like her to send a 'psychic' out to try and talk him into it.

"No. Like I said, I'm here looking for someone and don't worry, it's definitely not you," she said, appearing angry herself now.

Had she read his mind?

Alex shoved the insane idea out of his head. He wasn't about to fall for that mumbo-jumbo.

"I have to go. She's obviously not here. It must be the wrong time," mumbled Carissa, reaching into her pocket. She took out her truck keys and began walking back down the path.

"Wait!" he called out to her. "You're looking for a *woman?*"

Carissa glanced back at him over her shoulder. "No. A little girl."

Before he could ask her anything more, she was gone.

Chapter 2

CARISSA KNEW THAT Alex thought she was a flake. It didn't particularly bother her, however. She was used to it. As soon as she confided in anyone about her psychic abilities, they automatically assumed she was a fraud or a nut-job.

She got into her Tahoe and headed back to the cabin she'd rented in Castle Danger, which was less than two miles away. As she pulled into the parking lot of the resort, her cell phone rang.

"Hi, Mom."

"Hi, Carissa. Did you find out anything yet?"

Her mother was the only other person who knew she'd driven up to the North Shore and why.

"No."

"Have you had any more visions?"

"A little, but nothing substantial."

The only thing Carissa was sure of was that a little girl was going to be taken somewhere near Gooseberry Falls. And from the urgency she was feeling, it would be soon. In her visions, she'd seen the girl being chased by someone near the bottom of the falls. She sensed that her attacker had killed little girls before and the cops were looking in the wrong direction. It was another reason why she felt so compelled to do what she could to help.

"That's too bad. Are you sure you have the right place?"

"Yes. I knew the moment I pulled up yesterday."

She'd had her first vision almost a week ago, which had consisted of a young blonde girl, a white van, and a three-tiered waterfall. The following evening, she'd envisioned an endless lake, cargo ships, and a blizzard.

"But what if you're in the wrong state?"

"I'm not. Last night I dreamt of snow, which is on its way, and a license plate."

"A license plate? Now, that's a new one. You didn't happen to get the numbers, did you?" her mom asked dryly.

"No. They were a blur but it was definitely a Minnesota plate." It was frustrating, only getting bits and pieces at a time. But at least it was something.

"Well… I just hope you have the right waterfalls."

"I'm pretty confident that I'm in the right area, Mom."

After doing some research, Carissa found Gooseberry Falls, near Lake Superior. Driving three hours away had been a longshot, but once she'd arrived, everything felt right. Now, if she just knew more about the little girl. Or the monster in her visions.

"Maybe you should contact the police if everything is clicking into place for you," suggested her mother.

Carissa grunted. "They won't take me seriously, especially a small town like this. Remember the last time I tried talking to the authorities about Stephen Cutler?"

"But they found him because of you," she replied.

"Yes, but Detective Samuels thought it was just a coincidence."

Last summer, nine-year-old Stephen had been abducted while riding his bike home from a friend's house in the suburbs of Forest Lake, Minnesota. It had been around eight o'clock in the evening and the man who picked him up, Joe Phillips, had been a longtime neighbor. Stephen had trusted the man, so when he was told that his mother needed him to come home quickly because of a family emergency, the little boy hadn't thought twice about getting into his truck.

She wasn't even sure how or why she'd envisioned what would happen to that particular boy. It wasn't as if she'd come into any physical contact with him or his family, which usually triggered her premonitions. But, two hours after the boy had gone missing, an Amber Alert went out and she'd been watching television when they'd broadcasted it. The moment she saw the photo of Stephen, she immediately called the police.

"I know who has the little Cutler boy," she'd told the operator on the phone.

They'd immediately connected her to Detective Samuels, who was also a friend of the missing boy's family. When she told him of her vision, he'd immediately hung up on her. Knowing that it was a matter of life or death, she drove her SUV to the neighborhood where the search party was looking for the child, and was able to talk to the boy's uncle, Tim.

"There's a fifty-something-year-old man who lives in this neighborhood. He owns a white pickup truck and always wears a fishing hat," she'd told him desperately. "He's taking Stephen to his cabin."

"How do you know this?" the uncle had asked, skeptical.

"I saw him take the boy," she'd said, which had been both a lie and the truth. "You have to hurry and stop him before he kills your nephew. Believe me, he will if you don't do something."

Frantic, Tim called the boy's father, who knew exactly of whom she was talking about. Although the parents insisted that they trusted their neighbor, Carissa pleaded with them to find Joe Phillips. Desperate to locate their son, they called Samuels and insisted that he check out the lead. An hour later, Joe was pulled over on the interstate with Stephen Cutler unconscious in the backseat, unharmed, for the most part. When the police inspected Joe's cabin in Wisconsin, however, they found traces of blood in his basement, and later, the skeletal remains of another missing child, buried in the backyard. When interviewed later, Carissa admitted that she hadn't witnessed Joe take Stephen with her own eyes and that it had been a premonition. Grateful for getting their son back, Stephen's parents didn't care either way, nor could they thank her enough. Detective Samuels, on the other hand, didn't like her story, but couldn't connect her in any way to the perpetrator. In the end, he thanked her for 'the hunch' and informed Carissa that she might have to testify in court. It never happened, however. Joe Phillips died of a heart attack three weeks later, in his cell.

"A coincidence?" her mother said dryly. "I swear, everyone is so close-minded and afraid to take stock in anything they don't understand."

"I know," Carissa said, still thinking back to that case. "I guess I can't blame them totally. Sometimes I don't understand these things myself."

"The only thing you need to understand is that you've been given a gift."

She agreed, but the gift had taken a toll on her life. Every case exhausted her, and even though she was only twenty-eight, she sometimes felt closer to forty.

"I still don't like the idea that you're handling this on your own," grumbled her mother. "What if you get hurt?"

"Don't worry about me, Mother. I'll be fine."

"I knew you should have gotten your Carry-and-Conceal permit. Did you even bring your gun with you?"

She owned a Ruger and had only used it for target practice. She couldn't imagine pulling it on anyone. Her mother, on the other hand, was raised in a family of hunters and eventually married a police officer. She owned three of them herself and had taught Carissa how to fire a gun.

"No, I didn't bring it," she told her. "I did bring some pepper spray."

"Pepper spray?" she scoffed. "You should have brought the Ruger."

"I can't go waving guns at people, Mother. I'm not a cop. With my luck, I'd be the one getting arrested." The truth was, she'd been planning on bringing hers, but had been in such a hurry to get up to Duluth, she'd forgotten it. Even if she'd brought it along, however, it was unlikely she'd load the thing.

Her mother sighed. "You can't rely on those karate lessons. Not if this guy has a weapon."

Carissa had taken martial arts classes more for her own sanity than anything else. They helped her focus, and with her mind constantly receiving psychic impressions, it was a good distraction. It also helped keep her in shape.

"I'm aware of that."

"Are you a Black Belt yet?"

"No." She was almost there, though. Almost. "I'd have invited you to the graduation."

Her mother was silent on the other end of the phone.

"Mom, I'll be fine," Carissa said, trying to reassure her again.

"Is that what your psychic abilities are telling you?"

"Yes," she lied for her mother's benefit.

Carissa never had any premonitions about herself, but she wasn't a fool. She was trying to stop a dangerous man from killing a little girl. If she tried got in the way, he wasn't going to back away peacefully. If she didn't do something, however, the child would die.

"Thank goodness for that."

"I have to go," she told her, feeling guilty about lying but knowing it was the only way to comfort her mother. "I was just about grab a bite to eat."

"How is the cabin?"

"It's beautiful. I have a great view of Lake Superior," she told her, staring toward her front doorway. Her cabin was a one-bedroom, much smaller than the others, but cozy. It had a small kitchen, a fireplace, and a deck overlooking the lake. Behind the cabins were small fire-pits, where guests could relax at night, roast marshmallows, or simply enjoy the scenic views. Nothing she could take advantage of at the moment, but Carissa decided that one day, she'd like to return.

"I saw the pictures on the internet. It looks like a wonderful place to stay. Maybe I should drive up there…"

"Mom, I know you're busy this weekend. You said so yourself that you were going to be showing Betsy how to make strawberry rhubarb jam."

"That can wait a few more days."

Carissa frowned. "You're not following me up here. Besides, it's only a one bedroom cabin."

"So? I can sleep on the sofa. I've slept on worse."

It was useless arguing with her. She was a full-blooded, stubborn, no-nonsense Irish woman. Colleen Marie Jones had been widowed at thirty-two and had practically raised Carissa on her own. If she wanted to drive out, she would. "You know this might be a wild goose chase," said Carissa, trying to backtrack. "I could be out here wasting time."

"I don't believe that. Neither do you. You're supposed to be there. This is your calling in life and you're damn good at it."

Carissa knew it was, but there were times when she'd have traded her psychic abilities in for something else. Being able to see both the good and evil in people was very trying. "I know. It's just…I wish I knew more about the child or could see the man's face."

"Are you certain it's a man?"

"Yes," she replied. She didn't know how, but last night Carissa had somehow been able to tap into the man's psyche, and what she'd seen there had given her the chills. He was a very disturbed individual.

26

Chapter 3

Superior Views Resort
Castle Danger, Minnesota

"MOMMY, CAN WE go outside and look for rocks?" asked Chloe, staring out the window toward Lake Superior.

"Ask Daddy to take you out," said Rachel, unpacking the groceries. They'd rented the cabin for her best friend's wedding, and had decided to stay for a few extra days after the ceremony. "I'm a little too busy right now."

Chloe looked at her father, who was playing a game on his phone. As usual. "Daddy?"

"Hold on. Let me just finish this level," Paul said, not looking up.

Chloe groaned. "Can I just go out there myself? You can watch me through the window."

Rachel, listening in, frowned. Chloe was only seven years old. There was no way in hell she'd let her near the water without someone around to keep an eye on her. "I don't think that's a good idea. I don't want you out by the lake without one of us around."

"I won't go close to the water," pleaded Chloe. "I just want to look for rocks."

"Wait for your father," said Rachel, looking at Paul. Frustrated with his game obsession, her voice tightened. "He's *almost* finished."

Paul looked up from his game. "Yes, I am," he replied, not missing the irritation in Rachel's tone.

Chloe scowled and then her eyes lit up. "Look! Maddy is out there taking pictures. She can watch me."

Maddy was the bride-to-be, Mackenzie's, younger sister, who'd just turned twenty-two. She'd babysat Chloe a number of times and knew how precarious the child could be.

"I guess if she doesn't mind," murmured Rachel. She walked to the window and caught the younger woman's attention. They waved at each other.

"I'm going out by Maddy!" hollered Chloe, racing over to the doorway. She slipped on her shoes and was out the front door before Rachel could stop her.

***

"Hey, kiddo," said Maddy, taking a picture of a large barge that was making its way across the lake. "What's shaking?"

"Nothing. I'm just looking for rocks," said Chloe, skipping over to her. "What are you doing?"

"What does it look like I'm doing?" she replied, smiling at her in amusement.

"Taking pictures?"

"Yes. Do you see the barge over there?" Maddy said, pointing across the lake.

28

Chloe nodded and then began looking for rocks. After visiting the marine museum earlier in the day, she was bored with looking at boats.

Maddy, noticing her lack of enthusiasm for the ship, chuckled. "Not impressed, huh?"

She shrugged.

"I suppose you're a little young to appreciate stuff like that," said Maddy, taking one last picture. "Have you ever heard of the Edmund Fitzgerald?"

"Yes. We saw something about it at the boat museum," said Chloe. "It sunk."

"Yes, it did. It left Two Harbors, which is that way," said Maddy, pointing. "And was hit with a storm before it could reach its destination. Anyway, my grandfather was on that ship." She smiled sadly. "I guess he was a deckhand."

Chloe's eyes widened. "He was? Did he die?"

"Yes. Everyone died that day, unfortunately."

"Do you miss him?"

"Actually, I wasn't even born yet," replied Maddy. "My mother missed him terribly, though. So did my grandmother."

"That's so sad," said Chloe, still staring up at her.

She nodded. "Anyway, that's why my sister wanted to get married up here. It's where our grandparents grew up."

"That's cool. Oh… hey! Look at that rock," said Chloe, leaning down to pick it up. "It looks like it has stripes."

"It sparkles, too," Maddy said, staring at the black and white bands. "It's very pretty."

"It sure is," said a man's voice.

29

Chloe and Maddy turned to look at the stranger. He was a heavier-set man in his sixties, with a slight paunch, puffy white hair, and glasses.

"I think it's a gneiss," he continued, walking toward them.

"What's a gneiss?" asked Chloe.

"A foliated, metaphoric rock," he replied, smiling at them warmly. "Basically, it means that it's been exposed to heat and direct pressure, below the earth's surface. The lighter bands around it are made from feldspar and quartz. That's what makes them so intriguing."

"This one, too?" asked Chloe, picking up another rock that looked similar.

"Yes," he said.

"You certainly know a lot about rocks," said Maddy, noticing that he was also carrying a camera.

"I'm a high school science teacher," he said with a warm smile. "And part-time photographer. I should probably introduce myself." He held out his hand to Maddy. "My name is Harold Williams. I'm the photographer your sister hired for her wedding."

"Oh. I thought you looked familiar. She showed me your website," Maddy replied, shaking it.

"Oh, good. I also do holiday, family, high school, and children's portraits," he said and then turned to look at Chloe, who was busying herself with searching for more rocks. "Speaking of young people, who is this lovely little sprite?"

"That's Chloe," said Maddy. "Say hello to Mr. Williams."

Chloe looked over at him. "Hello."

"A rock hunter, huh? Are you a collector?" asked Harold.

Chloe nodded. "Yes. I'm bringing them home to remember our trip. It's the first one I've ever been on."

"Excellent idea. Where are you from?" he asked.

"Minnesota," replied Chloe.

Maddy and Harold both laughed.

"You're *in* Minnesota, silly," said Maddy. "Do you remember the city you live in?"

Chloe blushed. "Minneapolis."

"You don't have to be embarrassed," replied Harold. "Compared to Minneapolis, I imagine this place seems very far away."

She nodded. "It took us a gazillion hours to get here."

Chuckling again, he looked at Maddy. "I suppose at that age, it did feel like a gazillion hours. Is she your daughter?"

"No. She's a friend's," said Maddy.

"Ah. I thought you looked a little too young to have children," replied Harold.

"I actually have a very close friend, who is my age, with a five-year old son. He just started kindergarten."

"Ah, yes. Babes having babes. In any case, "he turned back toward Chloe, "she is a lovely child probably very photogenic. You know, I'm having a few specials going on in regards to family photos. I should ask her parents if they'd be interested in getting photographed while they're here."

"Yeah, you should. I know they'll be staying at the resort for a few extra days after the wedding tomorrow," she replied.

"Good to know. We could shoot some pictures near Gooseberry Falls. It's lovely there this time of year," he said.

31

"I bet," said Maddy. "I've yet to visit there. I'm hoping to stop on Sunday, before I head back to the Twin Cities."

"You should definitely not leave until you've checked it out. It's only a couple of miles up the road from here," he replied. "Although, it's supposed to start snowing soon. They say we'll get anywhere from three to ten inches. In the next couple of days, Gooseberry Falls will be covered with slow and pretty slippery."

"Yeah, I heard about the snow. My sister and our mother have been freaking out about it."

"I'm sure her wedding day will still be magical. Brides are always stressed out, even on the most beautiful of days," he replied.

"That's why I'm never getting married," said Maddy. "Or, if I do, I'm not having a big wedding. I'd rather run off to Vegas and elope."

"Nothing wrong with that," said Harold. "Do you have a beau right now?"

"Uh, kind of. It's a complicated situation," she replied.

"Too bad. A pretty young woman your age shouldn't have complications," he said.

"You can't always help who you fall in love with," she said, smiling sadly.

"No. I agree with you there wholeheartedly," said Harold.

"Chloe, don't go so close to the water," said Maddy.

"Sorry," she said, moving back toward them.

"So, Chloe, have you been to see the falls with your parents yet?"

"No," said Chloe, kneeling down to examine another rock she'd found. "But mommy said we're going in a couple of days."

Harold smiled. "You're in for a real treat. Especially being a rock enthusiast."

The back door of the cabin opened and Paul walked toward them, his hands in his pockets. Noticing the stranger standing there, he frowned slightly.

"Oh, hi, Paul," said Maddy.

"Hi," he replied, smiling warmly at her. "Thanks for keeping an eye on Chloe."

"No problem," she said.

"Daddy, look at the gnu that I found!" said Chloe, racing toward him with her rock held high.

"Gneiss," corrected Harold with a smile.

"Wow. Good find, sweetheart," said Paul, looking it over.

"Paul, this is Harold Williams," said Maddy. "He's shooting the wedding pictures."

"Nice to meet you," said Harold, offering his hand.

Paul shook it. "Nice to meet you, too."

"Your little girl is very photogenic. I was just telling Maddy about this sale we have going on. For family photos. If you're interested in having some professional pictures taken of you and your family while vacationing, I could give you a business card."

"To be honest, I don't think we'll have time for pictures," said Paul, "but thanks for the offer."

"Well, if you change your mind, I'll be around the next couple of days," he replied. "You know, shooting the wedding."

"Yeah. I'll let you know if we do," he said.

"Speaking of," said Maddy, looking at her watch. "We have the wedding rehearsal in two hours. I need to get moving."

"Us, too, I suppose," he replied. "Which cabin are you staying in, by the way?"

Maddy pointed down the row. "The third one from yours."

He nodded.

Maddy turned to Chloe. "Goodbye, sweetie. I'll see you at the rehearsal."

"Goodbye," she replied, wiping sand off of her hand and on onto her jacket.

"It was nice meeting you, Maddy," said Harold.

"You, too. See you later," she replied and then headed down the path toward her cabin.

"I suppose I should call my fiancée," said Harold, watching Maddy. "Before she wonders if I've fallen into the lake. I told her I was going to take some shots."

Paul turned to him. "Oh, you're engaged, too?"

He grinned. "Yes. We're getting married next summer."

Paul stared at him in surprise. Harold looked like he was pushing sixty-five or seventy. "Really? First one?"

"Marriage? No. Second. The first didn't work out so well," he replied.

"And you're willing to throw the dice again?" joked Paul. "You must be quite the gambler."

He chuckled. "I've learned over time that when you truly love someone, you have to be willing to do whatever it takes to be with them."

"I suppose," replied Paul.

Harold's phone buzzed. He took it out and read a text message. "Yep, she's getting anxious. I'd better call her back before she has a stroke."

"Impatient, huh? Hopefully she doesn't have her period, like mine does right now. Impatience is the least of my worries," he joked.

Harold smiled. "Thankfully, she hasn't had that problem for a few years."

"Lucky bastard. I guess that's one thing to look forward to when they get older," replied Paul, smirking. "No rag, no hag."

Harold snorted. "Well, I never thought of it that way, but then she has always been good-natured, even back when she had her monthly."

"What's a monthly?" asked Chloe, stuffing another rock into her pocket.

"Ask your mother," Paul replied, pulling his phone out. "But use extreme caution and don't tell her I told you to do it."

"Mommy said that I should never keep secrets from her," said Chloe with a serious expression.

"I think this is my cue to leave," said Harold, looking amused again. "I'll see you both soon, I'm sure."

Paul nodded.

"Goodbye, Chloe," said Harold. "Keep looking for rocks. There are some real gems around here."

"I will," she replied, not looking up from her rock expedition. "Bye."

With a last nod to Paul, the older man turned and walked away.

Chloe picked up a couple more stones and then started moving back down toward the shoreline.

"Hey. Stay over here where I can see you," said Paul, looking up from his cell. "Don't wander off."

Chloe scowled. "But, it's getting boring over here," she replied. "Can't we go for a walk?"

"No. We have to get in soon, anyway," he replied, his focus once again back on his phone.

Chloe was disappointed. "Are you playing that zombie game again?"

"No. I was just sending someone a message," he said, typing frantically.

"Who? Mommy?"

"No, a friend," he said, typing again.

Bored with her rock hunt, she walked over to her father. "Can I send a message to someone?"

Paul didn't look up. "Maybe later."

"I'm going back inside," huffed Chloe, irritated that he was ignoring her again. She stomped toward the cabin, her father oblivious to everything but the conversation on his cell phone.

Chapter 4

HE STOOD outside the main lodge, smoking a cigarette, when he saw the little blonde girl heading back to her cabin and looking frustrated. She glanced his way.

He smiled at her and waved.

She waved back hesitantly and went inside.

Faith.

They called her Chloe but by God, it was *her*. This time, there was no doubt in his mind. She was the right age and had the same features as his daughter. The eyes. The dimples. The rounded cheeks. Hell, even at one point, their eyes had met and he saw something reflected there.

Recognition?

It was possible. Barbara certainly didn't understand the bond between them. As much as she probably wanted to wipe Faith's memory clean of her father, she would never succeed. Not completely. He couldn't wait for them to be reunited so he could undo the brainwashing she'd been exposed to and be Faith's hero again.

He remembered a time when Faith was still in his life and he'd given her a scooter for her birthday. She'd been doing so well on it, but then fell down, skinning her knee. Barbara had tried soothing

37

her but it wasn't until he took her into his arms that she finally calmed down. Faith was a daddy's girl, through-and-through. He figured that it was another reason why Barbara had taken her. Pure jealousy.

He watched as the man staying with Faith walked around the cabin and went inside. He didn't like the guy, and from the expression on Faith's face, he'd said or done something to make her angry. He wondered who the couple really were and hoped to hell that Barbara wasn't going to be at the wedding. Most of the guests staying there were part of it. The last thing he needed was for the bitch to recognize him before he had a chance to grab Faith. He couldn't do it until then, not without the risk of getting caught. He needed to wait until the reception. It would be much easier when everyone was drunk and relaxed.

Taking another drag of his smoke, he smiled again at his luck. He couldn't believe that this time, fate had brought his daughter to him, especially after such a harrowing week. The last girl, the soccer player, had been yet another catastrophe. Just thinking about it made him sick to his stomach.

Damn you, Barbara.

He should have known that the girl, Amy, had been too old. But, she'd looked so much like his daughter and had played soccer like a champ. God, he'd wanted so much for her to be Faith. But, just like the last two, she'd been a mistake.

"Please... let me go."

Amy's last words echoed in his head. He pictured her lifeless eyes, staring toward the sky after he did what he had to do. Like the others, he'd cried afterward, consumed by guilt. But, it couldn't be helped. She'd seen him without his disguise and had even recognized him as a coach from the other school. If he would have let her go, she would have ratted him out. So, he was left with little choice – kill Amy and create a crime scene that would throw the cops off. He'd watched his share of C.S.I. shows to know how to do it, too. The first was to make sure they never found a weapon, which is why he always used his bare hands to do the dirty work. No risk of leaving a gun or knife behind. Plus, blood made him queasy and guns were traceable. It wasn't as if he knew of anyone selling illegal firearms. Admittedly, squeezing the last breath out of the girls had been horrible; he felt like less of a monster knowing that it didn't give him any thrills.

I did what I had to do.

He shuddered, thinking about how he'd removed Amy's clothing to set the stage for the cops. He wanted the authorities to think he was a deviant. A sexual predator. The thought of touching her intimately had made him physically ill, though, and that's where he'd drawn the line. But, he'd made sure to pose her in a position that would make them think he was a pedophile. He was no sicko, though. Just a desperate man who wanted his daughter back.

"Not your fault," he reminded himself, stubbing out his cigarette.

Trying to forget the victims, rather *Barbara's* victims, he pushed the horrible memories away and headed into the main lodge.

Chapter 5

CARISSA DECIDED TO eat an early dinner at Blue Waters, the resort's restaurant. As she was being seated, she noticed that the bar area was busy.

"This place is hopping," she said to the waitress, when she brought her a glass of ice water.

"Yeah. There's a wedding tomorrow and the rehearsal is tonight," explained the woman. "Are you part of that group?"

"No. I guess it's a good thing I arrived here when I did," Carissa replied, opening up the menu. "Beat the rush."

"Yes, it's going to be very busy. Especially the bar. Speaking of which, can I get you anything other than water to drink?"

As much as she would have enjoyed a small glass of wine, Carissa hesitated. She was alone and not there to relax. She also needed all of her wits about her.

"We have half-priced cocktails right now," the waitress added.

"I'm good. Thank you."

"No problem. I'll be back in a few minutes to take your order."

"Thank you."

The waitress left and Carissa scanned the menu, deciding on a bowl of chicken and wild-rice soup with a side salad. Closing the menu, she noticed one of the bartenders checking her out. He was handsome and athletic looking, with dark blond hair and crinkly blue eyes. She guessed him to be around her age, late twenties.

He smiled at her.

She smiled back and then quickly busied herself on her cell phone. She sensed he was attracted to her and was flattered but not interested.

When the waitress returned, she ordered her food and handed the woman back the menu.

"So, do a lot of people get married here?" asked Carissa, pushing her hair behind her ears.

"Yeah, but not so much this time of the year. We see a lot more weddings in the warmer months."

"I imagine," Carissa said, looking through the large-paned window next to her booth. A few light flakes were beginning to fall from the sky and the view, which overlooked the lake, was beautiful. She could definitely see how one would want to have an outdoor wedding there.

"So, where did you say you were from?" the waitress asked.

She told her.

"Ah. I've never been out of Duluth. I've been meaning to take a trip down to the Twin Cities."

"There are a lot of great places to explore in St. Paul and Minneapolis."

"I've always wanted to check out the Mall of America. Is it as big as they say?"

"Oh, yeah. It's an all day excursion, and that's not counting the theme park inside."

She smiled. "Sounds cool."

"It is. Although," Carissa looked outside again, "to be honest, I'm more fascinated with what's up here. I just love the North Shore."

"Me, too. I wouldn't want to live any other place. Well, maybe Hawaii."

"Have you ever been there?" asked Carissa.

"No."

"It's a nice place to visit, but here is better. Take my word for it," she replied, having visited Honolulu. It was indeed lovely, but too busy for her.

The waitress smiled. "Well, I'd better go put your order in before you starve to death. Let me know if I can get you anything else."

"Okay, thanks."

The waitress left and Carissa glanced toward the bar area again. It had picked up quite a bit during the last few minutes. Most of them seemed to know each other, so she assumed they were guests of the bride and groom. Carissa studied the small crowd, wondering if one of them might know the little girl she was looking for. Of course, it was always possible that the child was a local, too, or staying at a different resort. If only she could reach out and touch everyone without looking like a total nut-job. It would save so much time.

Sighing, Carissa's mind went back to her own childhood. From early on, she had known things. Things she shouldn't have known and things she couldn't explain. Growing up, Carissa chalked everything up as being strange coincidences or lucky guesses. It wasn't until she was a freshman in college that she'd learned of her psychic abilities. She'd been at a Halloween frat party. Not really much of a drinker herself during that time, she'd stayed sober and so her mind had been clear. Halfway through the night, a tipsy young man, wearing a freaky clown mask, had bumped into her, almost knocking her over. He'd reached out to steady her and the moment his hand touched arm, Carissa was instantly hit with a premonition – it was of him slipping something into a girl's drink and then raping her afterward. It had disturbed her so much that she'd kept an eye on him for most of the night. Eventually, Carissa brushed off the vision, thinking it was from lack of sleep and an overactive imagination. Nothing happened and she left the party with her friends. Ten days later, she learned that the guy under the clown mask had been Daryl Huppert and he'd been arrested for the very thing she'd envisioned. The only difference was that he'd committed the crime at another frat party the following weekend. She'd been off by a week. The experience had shaken her, and from that moment on, she read everything she could on the subject of clairvoyance and extrasensory perception.

"Hey, Ben, could you turn up the television?" asked one of the men sitting at the bar.

"Sure, Mac," said the handsome bartender. He grabbed the remote and turned up the volume.

Carissa looked at the television and noticed that a reporter was standing in front of a sign that read *North Heights Ski Resort*.

"Earlier today, a child's body was discovered on one of the mountains here at the North Heights Ski Resort, in Lutsen, Minnesota. Officials haven't released any information about the girl's identity yet, only that foul play is suspected."

Horrified, Carissa's breath caught in her throat. She'd been too late.

"Isn't that just an hour from here?" asked one of the other guests seated at the bar.

"Yeah," replied Ben. "Pretty scary, huh?"

"Jesus, what kind of a freak would do something like that to a little girl?" Barry muttered, scowling at the television.

"Listen," said Ben, turning the volume up higher.

"Has anyone at the resort filed a report about a missing child?" asked the anchorman, with a grave expression.

The camera zoomed back to the reporter.

She shook her head. "Apparently not. It's a slow time of the year for the resort, though, the manager said."

"Well, there hasn't been a lot of snow," said the anchorman. "Thank you, Joanna. Please keep us updated. This is such a horrible tragedy."

"It is. I'll keep you posted," she replied.

The anchorman looked at the camera. "Speaking of weather, let's check in with Jim Sanchez for an update on this weekend's forecast."

"I hope they find out who did this and catch the bastard," said Barry.

"It's probably someone traveling to Canada," said Ben.

"Or maybe from Canada." Barry sighed. "These wackos don't usually do things like this in their own backyard."

The child was from Duluth, thought Carissa, closing her eyes. She tried envisioning the girl, wondering if it was the one from her dreams. Something told her that it wasn't, but there was definitely a correlation.

"Here you go," said the waitress.

Carissa opened up her eyes as the woman placed her soup and salad on the table.

"Thank you."

"You're welcome. Is there anything else I can get you?"

She knew what she had to do and that it was going to be a long night. "Yes, actually. Can I get a cup of coffee?" asked Carissa.

Chapter 6

AN HOUR LATER, after changing into a pair of blue jeans and hiking boots, Carissa was on the road and heading toward Lutsen. Unfortunately, it was a few degrees colder than earlier and the snow was starting to accumulate, making it irritatingly slippery.

Turning on the windshield wipers, Carissa's mind drifted back to Gooseberry Falls. She'd been so sure that something was going to happen at that location. Of course, there was still the chance that the killer was going to strike there as well.

Or, maybe the child was killed in Gooseberry Falls and driven up to Lutsen?

Whatever the case, Carissa knew that she'd get some answers at the ski resort. Hopefully, they'd be the kind that would help her find a killer.

***

Thirty minutes into the drive, Carissa decided to stop for gas and use a restroom. She pulled into the parking lot of a convenience store in Little Marais. After filling her tank, she went inside to pay, and found herself face-to-face with Alex, the DNR officer. He was on his way out, holding a six-pack of beer and a plastic bag filled with what looked like half a dozen frozen pizzas.

Alex grinned. "You, again? Don't tell me – your psychic senses told you I'd be here and you wanted to apologize for leaving so abruptly?"

Carissa blushed. She had taken off quickly, but he'd made her uncomfortable. "No. Sorry... I was just in the area and needed gas."

"Ah. So, you're visiting out this way?" he asked, his eyes probing hers.

"Still asking questions. Aren't you off duty?" she teased, nodding toward the beer.

"I am now. I was just about to go home and throw in a pizza. You're welcome to join me, if you'd like."

Her eyes widened at his blunt request.

"Sorry," he said, smiling sheepishly. "I didn't mean like a 'date' or anything. I just figured you might want to talk. You know, about that girl you were searching for? Did you ever find her?"

"No," she said, moving out of the way for another customer. "Unfortunately."

"Speaking of missing children, I don't know if you've watched the news," he said, lowering his voice. "But, they discovered a child's body up in Lutsen."

"I know. Actually, I'm headed up there right now, in fact–" She stopped and her throat tightened as a sudden, clear image of the victim popped into her head.

"Carissa?"

The girl's clothes had been removed, but not because she'd been molested.

47

"Hey. Are you okay?" asked Alex, stepping closer.

Carissa snapped out of it. "Yeah. Sorry."

"Another premonition?"

"I need to go," she replied, avoiding eye contact. She needed to be alone to see if she could pick up on anything else.

He frowned. "Now? Are you really sure you want to go up there? It's dark and the roads are getting slippery."

She brushed some hair out of her eyes and sighed. "I don't care. I've come this far and am not about to let a little snow get in my way."

Alex wanted to grill Carissa with questions, but even now she looked like a frightened rabbit, ready to bolt.

"I just returned from the crime scene myself. With all of the cops and media, you won't get close."

Hard determination filled her eyes. "I have to try."

"Why?"

Another customer walked in and Carissa had to move out of the way again. "I can't talk about it in here."

"Then I'll meet you outside," he replied.

Her eyes narrowed. "Fine. But, I don't want you mocking me again."

"I won't. I swear." He grinned. "Hell, I might even give you the benefit of the doubt."

"How generous of you," she said a little dryly.

"Just give me a chance."

She relaxed. "Fine. I'll be right out."

"Okay."

Alex walked outside to his vehicle, which was parked at one of the pumps. He put his groceries into the back of his Jeep Cherokee and waited for her.

A few minutes later, Carissa stepped out of the gas station and headed in his direction.

"Brrr," she said, sliding her hands into her pockets as she approached his vehicle.

"I know and it's going to be even colder tomorrow. The roads are getting worse by the minute," he said, watching as a car almost spun out on the road next to them.

"Yeah. They are."

"So, this must be about your missing girl. Do you think it's her?"

"I don't know for sure," she replied. "And that's why I need to see her body, or at the very least, get close to the crime scene."

"The police aren't going to allow that. They've got their forensic team up there now, collecting evidence. It's all blocked off."

"They won't be there all night. I'll just wait for them to finish up and then do what I need to do," she said stubbornly.

Alex sighed. "It could be a long night."

"I don't care. I know you think I'm some kind of crazy woman—"

"Hold on now, I never said that," he said, frowning.

"No, but you were thinking it earlier."

She had a point. He still didn't believe in mediums or psychics, but it was obvious that Carissa was very serious about trying to find her missing girl, and he certainly respected her tenacity. Something told him that she'd wait all night to get what she needed.

"I should go." She turned and began walking toward the black Tahoe parked behind his. "Have a good night," she said coolly.

"Hold on a second," he replied, following her.

Carissa turned around.

"Hell, I don't have anything better to do. Why don't I drive you out there? I know some of the guys investigating the case. I might be able to persuade them to let you get close enough to do your…" he rubbed his chin and smiled, "whatever it is that you psychics do."

Her eyebrow rose. "So, you really are going to give me the benefit of the doubt? Amazing."

"Yeah, but under one condition."

"The condition that I don't 'read' you?"

He stared at her in surprise.

"Don't look so alarmed," Carissa replied, amused. "You have a horrible poker face. You'd be an easy target for someone to take advantage of. Especially those hokey fortunetellers."

He laughed.

Chapter 7

AFTER GETTING PERMISSION from the gas station to leave her vehicle in the lot, Carissa climbed into Alex's Jeep.

"What about your pizza and beer?" she asked, buckling her seatbelt.

He took off his gloves and threw them onto the dashboard. "Actually, I just live a mile up the road. Would you mind if I dropped my things off there before we head up there? I need to let my dog out, too."

An image of a Golden Retriever flashed through her head and then trees.

"No problem. What's his name?" she replied, grateful that Alex was driving in the first place. The snow was starting to accumulate heavily and she'd yet to see a plow.

"Woody."

"Nice. I love dogs. Especially Goldens. They're such lovable animals."

Alex looked at her and his lip twitched. He turned his attention back to the road. "Yes. Mine would lick someone to death before ever trying to harm them."

"I bet."

"Do you have any pets?"

"I have a cat."

"What's your cat's name?"

Carissa pictured her white Persian. "Madame B."

"What does the 'B' stand for?"

"Bitch." Carissa smiled. "She's not always very friendly. She's getting better in her old age, but we've had quite a rocky relationship."

Alex chuckled. "Oh, yeah? A moody cat, huh?"

"Let's just say that when I get back home, she'll have expressed her irritation with me by wrecking something personal of mine. The last time she peed on a sweater that had fallen off of a hanger. The time before that, it was a shoe. A new one. She's not only a bitch, but a very smart one."

He laughed again. "She only does it when you're traveling?"

Carissa nodded. "Yes. I'd bring her with, but she'd be even angrier with me, I think."

"Maybe she's lonely and needs a companion?"

Carissa snorted. "Cats aren't like dogs. At least mine isn't. She likes her solitude but still needs me around when it suits her. When I'm not, she's very expressive."

"Sounds like my ex," he said dryly.

Knowing that it was a sore subject, Carissa didn't reply. Instead, she turned the subject back to Woody. "Dogs are very loyal. I've often thought about getting one," she said, as they headed toward a vehicle that must have spun out before ending up in a ditch. A tow-truck was on the scene and it was obvious that his night had just started.

"Even with Madame B?" he asked, slowing down as they went around the tow truck.

"Yes. It would serve her right."

"What's your hesitation?"

"My traveling. It would probably need to be kenneled or my mother would have to take care of it, and she's busy enough as it is. It wouldn't be fair to either of them."

"So, there isn't a significant other in your life to help out?"

Carissa's thoughts turned to Dustin, a man who she'd dated on-and-off in the last couple of years. He'd been an ex-cop turned private investigator, who'd first approached her after finding out about her psychic gifts. Dustin had been trying to locate a couple's seventeen-year-old daughter. They'd thought she'd been kidnapped until Carissa's involvement told them otherwise. She'd learned that Tina, the daughter, had run away with a boyfriend whom her parents had forbidden her to see the year before. She'd been secretly dating him and once the teenagers had saved up enough money, they'd taken off together. With that information, Dustin had found the couple in Vegas. The parents were reunited with Tina, who went home without much persuasion. Apparently, they'd been right about the boyfriend - he'd been pressuring her into becoming a hooker to pay for a drug habit she'd been too blinded by love to see. Afterward, Dustin had asked Carissa out and they'd started seeing each other, but then she'd started having premonitions about him. Ones he didn't want to hear about.

"Not right now," she replied, thinking about the last time she'd seen Dustin. They'd gotten into a huge fight after she'd tried warning him about getting shot. She'd had a vision of him taking a bullet during one of his cases.

"I appreciate your concern, but this is my life. It's who I am. I can't walk away because you have a 'feeling' that I'm going to get hurt," he'd argued.

"Even if it means getting murdered?"

"You said so, yourself – 'the future isn't set in stone, even after you get a glimpse of what could be'."

"Yes, but—"

"I always knew the dangers of being a cop and I certainly know that I'm not out of the woods as a P.I. If anything, some of the cases I take are more dangerous. But I can't give up my career to dodge a bullet that might not ever happen. You, of all people, should know why."

Dustin's older sister, Taylor, had been kidnapped and murdered while riding her bike home from a friend's house. She'd been nine and Dustin had been fourteen at the time. There'd been no witnesses and the police never caught the perpetrator. Dustin had been devastated, not only by the fact that he'd lost his little sister, but in the end, he ended up losing his parents as well. Wallowing in their grief, they'd blamed each other for Taylor's death while turning to alcohol to cope with the pain. Unfortunately, all Dustin could do was watch from the sidelines as their grief consumed the couple and they took for granted the son they still had. The experience left him an angry, distant teenager and then later, a determined young man who went into law enforcement. He spent the next few years as a cop, until one night, he met up with an old friend from high school, Joanna Mitchell, who was a private investigator. They started a personal relationship and eventually, Dustin gave up his badge and they became business partners, too. Unfortunately, things didn't work out for them romantically and they went their separate ways. Dustin then started up his own investigative business and eventually it brought him to Carissa.

"I suppose you intimidate a lot of men," Alex said, smiling.

"Why? Because of my psychic abilities?"

"I was going to say because you're very attractive, but once they find out you can read their minds, I'm sure that might send them running for the hills."

"I can't read minds," she said, ignoring the compliment about her looks. Carissa wasn't sure how she felt about it. Sure, it was flattering and he wasn't sore on the eyes either, but this was all about business and she didn't want it to turn into anything else. "I read energy."

"What do you mean?"

"Thoughts and feelings have energy. I can sometimes interpret the meanings behind certain energetic vibrations and get a feel for what someone *might* be thinking."

"Interesting. So, if you were standing next to a criminal or murderer, would you know?"

"Maybe. It depends on their energy and whether or not they were able to somehow block me from what they were truly feeling."

"Does that actually happen?"

"I guess I don't really know," she replied, smiling. "Most people that I've met are easy to read."

"What about me?"

"I thought you didn't want me to read you."

He laughed. "Good point. Enough about me. How did you find out about this little girl you're searching for?"

"Through my dreams," she replied, staring into the darkness as the image returned to her. The girl had blue eyes and long, dishwater blonde hair.

"How old?"

"I think somewhere between five and seven. It's hard to say."

"So, you drove all the way out here because of a dream you had about a child you've never met before?" he, said, turning down a dirt road.

"Yes. A little girl and a serial killer. The problem is, I can't see his face and I don't know anything about him, other than he'll end up murdering her if I don't stop him,"

"Do you know why he is doing this? Other than he's a sick bastard."

Noting the fact that Alex really *was* giving her the benefit of the doubt, she relaxed, closed her eyes, and tried thinking about the girl from her dreams. Instead, she was met with a new vision. It was the same man, but a different child, and he was furious.

She wasn't the one.

It had been a waste of time…

Carissa opened her eyes. "Oh, my God."

"What is it?"

"I think I know what he wants," she said, her stomach recoiling at the new knowledge. This wasn't the first girl he'd killed, and it wouldn't be the last. She looked at him. "He's searching for his daughter."

***

When they reached Alex's, he asked her if she'd like to meet Woody.

"Sure," she said, staring ahead at the charming, fenced-in cedar cabin. "Nice place, by the way."

He grinned. "Thank you. It's not huge, but now that it's just me and Woody, it's all we need."

She followed him up the steps, to the porch, and could hear his dog barking frantically from inside. "It might be small, but you can definitely add on later. How many acres do you have?"

"Ten," he said, unlocking the front door. "Get ready. Woody has a lot of energy."

"I bet," she replied as the happy dog rushed Alex, excited that his master was home.

"How's my buddy?" asked Alex, petting the wiggly Golden.

Carissa glanced around the living room, which opened up to the kitchen, and was impressed. Dark hardwood floors, a floor-to-ceiling stone fireplace, and marbled countertops in what looked to be a newly updated kitchen. It was a lovely home and she had a feeling that he'd kept his mind off of his ex-wife by doing some remodeling.

"Oh, hey there," she said, laughing as Woody moved to her next and began sniffing and licking her hands.

"I'm going to put this stuff into the kitchen. Could you take him outside? I'll be out in a minute."

"Of course," she replied. "Come on, Woody."

The dog followed her outside and began running through the snow, excited. After a few minutes, Alex stepped out of the house.

"Woody loves the first snowfall of the season," he said, watching as the dog raced back toward them, its tongue hanging out.

"I see that," she said, smiling.

Alex threw a tennis ball out into the yard and Woody went to go chase it down. He brought it back to him and they played the game a few more times until Alex looked at his watch. "It's getting late. We should probably go. Did he do his thing?"

"Yeah, I believe so," replied Carissa, rubbing her hands together.

"Woody! Come on, boy."

Not wanting to go in right away, the dog ran around the yard a few times before finally obeying. Afterward, they put him back inside the house and Alex dried the snow off of him before they left.

"He's a nice dog," she said, as they got back into the Jeep.

"Thanks. He's... really the only family I have left."

Something told her that it wasn't exactly the truth, but she didn't want to pry.

Alex pulled out a bag of beef jerky from the glove compartment. "Sorry, I have to eat something or I'm going to be a real grouch," he explained, holding out the bag to her. "Would you like any?"

"No thank you. I just ate dinner."

"Lucky you," he said, grabbing a piece of jerky. "I haven't eaten since lunchtime."

She stopped. "I'm sorry. You know, you don't have to drive me out there."

"I know, but at this point, I need to. Just for my own curiosity."

Carissa smiled. "As in what I might tell you about the case that the cops don't already know?"

"Exactly."

"I hope I don't disappoint you."

"Something tells me you won't," he said and smiled.

Chapter 8

HE'D BEEN SHOCKED to learn that the police had found Amy's body so quickly. Knowing that they were up there right now, collecting evidence and questioning people, made him anxious. Even though he'd tried his best not to leave anything behind, there was always the chance that he'd missed something. Or that someone had seen him drive away. He began to wonder if he should try and grab Faith tonight, instead of waiting until the following night. He could try and do it after the wedding rehearsal and dinner.

But how?

He wasn't sure. He didn't have his van, but he had some chloroform in the trunk of his car.

What to do… What to do…

If only Barbara hadn't put him in this situation.

He thought about the woman he'd once loved and how she'd changed so dramatically. One moment, they were a loving, happy couple with a young child. The next, she was being difficult and blamed everything on him.

"You keep forgetting to take your pills," she'd said. "And I feel like I'm always walking on eggshells around you."

"I'm sorry. I'll do better. I forget sometimes. You know I'd never hurt you."

Unfortunately, even when he remembered to take his medication, things between them didn't seem to get any better and he began to blame her friends. It was obvious that most of the busybodies didn't like him. He could see it in their eyes and knew they were probably feeding her bullshit about how she deserved better. Eventually, he demanded that she get new ones, which she refused to do. Then one night, Barbara told him that she had to work late. She was a loan officer at a bank and claimed that a client was coming in after hours to sign some paperwork. It sounded a little fishy, so he drove by the bank and noticed that her car wasn't there. When Barbara arrived home later that night, he confronted her and she confessed to lying.

"I went to see a lawyer. I'm leaving you," she'd declared.

He'd been shocked. "Why?"

"Because you frighten me, even when you take your pills. I'm afraid for myself and Faith."

He told her that she'd been overreacting and vowed he'd never harm either of them. Unfortunately, she had still wanted out.

"But, I love you, Barbara."

"I'm sorry, but I've fallen out of love with you."

Her words had cut him like a knife and he'd been heartbroken. *"You're not taking Faith from me."*

"You can see her every other weekend."

That set him off, and even with his pills, his temper got the best of him. He snapped and began screaming at her that he'd rather die than lose Faith.

"I'm not taking her away from you!" she'd cried. "She just won't be living in the same house with you."

To him there wasn't much of a difference. He wanted to wake up every morning and see her sunny face. He *needed* to be able to kiss her goodnight before she went to bed and not just every other weekend.

"No. You can leave me if you want to, but you're not taking my daughter."

"You're being irrational."

"I'm being irrational?!" He'd grabbed her by the neck and began to squeeze. *"You try taking my daughter and you'll see what irrational is really about."*

"Please... stop," she'd begged, staring at him with a horrified expression.

The rest was a bit of a blur, but in the end, she'd backed down and promised to be a better wife.

Obviously, she'd lied.

Now, he knew better than to trust anyone completely, especially women, and to go with his gut instincts. Right now, they were telling him that his time was running out and he needed to move quickly.

Chapter 9

"HONEY, GO AND change your clothes," said Rachel, peeking her head into Chloe's bedroom, where she was playing on her tablet. "It's time to go to the rehearsal."

Chloe looked up. "Can I wear my dress?" She was excited to put on the beautiful, pale blue satin gown her mother had purchased for the wedding. She loved spinning in it and couldn't wait to show it off.

"No, honey. That's for tomorrow. Wear something else. Something *clean.*" Rachel pointed at Chloe's top. "The shirt you have on has ketchup on it."

Chloe stared down at the stain and her lip started to quiver. There was a picture of a kitty on it and it was one of her favorites. "Oh no! I love this shirt. Will it come out?"

Rachel walked over and examined it. "Yes. I think so. Once you take it off, I'll try getting it out with hot water. Now, why don't you go and put on that white sweater that I bought you."

Although it wasn't as nice as the dress, Chloe loved the soft, fuzzy sweater and had forgotten about it. "Okay. You look so pretty, Mommy," she said, staring at her mother.

Rachel had changed into a pair of black slacks and a red silk blouse. She'd also applied makeup and had curled her dark blonde hair. It was rare to see her mother looking so nice.

"Thank you, sweetie," she replied, kissing the top of her head.

"She does look nice," agreed Paul, stepping into the bedroom. He'd also changed into a pair of dark pants and light blue dress shirt.

"Thank you," replied Rachel looking pleased.

"So, what time are we supposed to be there?" asked Paul, looking at his watch.

"In twenty minutes. Let's get you changed," Rachel said to Chloe.

Fifteen minutes later, all three had their winter jackets and boots on and were heading toward the main lodge, where the rehearsal was to take place. It was dark and the snow was falling rapidly. Although Chloe's parents grumbled about the weather, she was excited and already counting down the days before Christmas.

"Good thing we got up here when we did," said Paul. I'm sure the roads are already getting bad and some people are driving like idiots."

Rachel agreed.

Chloe stopped, tilted her head upward, and stuck out her tongue to capture a snowflake. She caught one and then another.

"Come on, kiddo," said Paul, noticing that she was lagging behind. "We're running late."

"Did you know that no two snowflakes are alike?" said Chloe, as he walked back to grab her hand. "That's what Mommy says."

"Well, then it must be true," he replied dryly as they began walking again.

"Can we go sledding?" Chloe asked.

"We're not here for that," he replied. "Besides, we don't have the gear."

"Can we do it when we get back home?" she asked, trying to keep up with her father, who was walking very quickly.

"Maybe. We'll see," he replied.

"You probably won't," she mumbled. Her father was always too busy.

"I said 'we'll see'. The snow might be melted by the time we get home, anyway," he said as they caught up to Rachel.

"What was that?" asked Rachel.

"I told Daddy that I wanted to go sledding when we get back home," explained Chloe.

"Sounds like fun," replied her mother. "Maybe we can even go tubing while we're up here? Mackenzie mentioned that there's a place not far from the resort where we can rent them. What do you think?"

Chloe's eyes lit up. "Could we really, Mommy? That would be so much fun."

"We can try. We'll look into it on Sunday, okay?" said Rachel, smiling warmly at her.

Paul sighed. "Honestly, I doubt we'll be getting *that* much snow."

"We're supposed to get several inches over the weekend," said Rachel, opening up the door to the lodge. "If you'd peel your eyes away from your phone once in a while and watch the weather report, you'd know that."

Paul rolled his eyes. "Don't start," he muttered as they stepped inside.

Sighing, Rachel walked up to the front desk and the attendant directed them to the courtyard.

"Just take those steps and you'll follow the hallway around to where they have everything set up," said the receptionist, pointing.

"Thank you," said Rachel.

"An outdoor wedding? Really? This should be fun," said Paul dryly as they took the staircase down.

"I'm sure they didn't anticipate a snow storm," said Rachel. "Anyway, it's not that cold and I think the snow is kind of pretty."

"Me, too," said Chloe. "When I grow up, I want to have a wedding outdoors, too. Do you think Santa and Mrs. Claus were married outside?"

Rachel smiled at her. "I imagine they were. They probably wanted the reindeer to join in the fun."

"And the elves, too," replied Chloe, now skipping ahead of them.

"Slow down and wait for us," called Rachel.

Chloe ignored her and kept going.

"Good. I'm not the only one running late," said Maddy, coming up behind them.

Rachel turned and smiled. "Hi, Maddy. Wow, you look really nice."

Maddy, who was holding her coat, had on a tight-fitting dark green dress that showed off her narrow waist, and black strappy heels. Her hair was in a chignon and she wore a black velvet choker with an emerald dangling down the middle.

"Thank you," she answered and then looked down at her heels. "My feet are going to be hating the snow, but hopefully, we won't be out in the cold for too long."

"I'm sure the rehearsal won't be long," said Rachel, glancing at her shoes.

Maddy looked at Paul and smiled. "Hi."

"Hi, Maddy," he replied. He gave her an appraising look as they stopped at the door. "You know, you're not supposed to outshine your sister this weekend. She's going to be ticked."

She laughed. "Thank you. I guess?"

"Obviously, Chloe's already outside," said Rachel, opening up the door leading to the courtyard.

"Of course," said Paul. "She's always on her own agenda."

Chapter 10

WHEN ALEX AND Carissa finally reached Lutsen, there were only a handful of investigators left at the crime scene, including Sheriff Jim Collins. Fortunately, Alex was friends with the man, and they were allowed to observe what was happening from a short distance away.

"So, what made you drive all the way back here, Richardson? And, in *this* shitty weather?" asked the sheriff, lighting a cigarette. He was a tall man, somewhere in his fifties, with probing eyes, sharp features, and a voice that reminded Carissa a little bit of Sam Elliot.

It took him several seconds to answer and she knew that he was worried about what the sheriff would think if he told him the truth. "I brought along a profiler, Jim. This is Carissa Jones. I think she might be able to help."

"No offense, but that's what we have forensics for," he replied, nodding toward the two men still evaluating the taped off area where the child had been found. It was hard to see much of anything because of the snow, and it was obvious they had their work cut out for them.

"I realize that. She's not your average profiler, though, and I figured that with a case like this, you could use all the help you can get," he replied.

The sheriff looked at her. "Where you from?"

"The Twin Cities," she replied.

"Ah. How'd you drive up here so fast?" he asked, taking another drag of his cigarette.

"I–"

Before she could finish her sentence, Alex cut in. "She came up here to visit me. We're... dating. Online."

Jim looked surprised. "Online dating? *You?*"

Alex looked embarrassed. "What can I say? A man gets lonely and bored."

"I get that. I'm just surprised, is all. So, this is your first date and you brought this pretty little lady here. To a crime scene." The sheriff chuckled. "Your mother needs to knock you upside your head."

Carissa couldn't help but smile. "Actually, we were going to have a lovely dinner and then I saw the news and wanted to help," she said, feeling bad for Alex. "He tried talking me out of it, but something tells me this killer is going to strike again. If I can help prevent that, it's worth skipping a romantic evening."

"I sure as hell hope that we don't have a serial killer in our midst," said Jim, his face darkening. "But, with the luck I've been having, you might just be onto something. So, Ms. Jones, you have identification? I can't just divulge information to anyone with a pretty face. Being a profiler, I imagine you work for the FBI?"

"Actually, I don't," she replied, looking at Alex helplessly and then back at the sheriff. "I pretty much just do this on the side."

"You're shitting me? On the *side*?" he replied and then looked at Alex. "You know I can't give out information like this to the general public. Hell, I probably shouldn't even allow you here, Alex."

"The girl that you found, she had blonde hair and blue eyes." Carissa closed her eyes, to try and be more receptive. Now, more than anything, she needed to prove herself.

"What's she doing?" asked Jim.

"Not sure," admitted Alex.

Blocking them out, she opened her mind and asked for help, this time from the spirit world. It was risky, opening herself up like that. She'd learned of other psychics getting duped by evil entities, and usually refrained from trying to go that route. But she wanted so much to find the child's killer.

Show me what happened…

She was rewarded with a vision. A horribly, violent one that made her shudder.

"What's wrong?" asked Alex.

She opened her eyes and blinked back tears that she didn't even know she had. "The man strangled her, thus the bruises around her throat. She was positioned in a lewd way and wore only… shin guards and soccer knee-highs."

"What the hell?" said Jim, shocked. "How'd you know all of that?"

She sighed. "I was shown. I also know she's from Duluth."

Jim looked at Alex.

"Don't look at me. I didn't tell her anything. I didn't even get to see the body," said Alex.

The sheriff put his cigarette out. "Ma'am, nobody knew any of this except for the officers here tonight, and the perp. I'm going to have to bring you in for questioning."

Chapter 11

WHEN THEY STEPPED outside, there were twenty or so people standing around and chatting. Sure enough, Chloe had already found Mackenzie and her fiancé, Brock, and was talking up a storm.

"Hi. Sorry we're late," said Rachel, walking over to them. They were standing by the archway, overlooking the lake. An older man was also with them, holding a camera and smiling at what Chloe was saying.

"It's not a problem," said Mackenzie. "By the way, have you met our photographer, Harold?"

"We've met," said Paul, sticking his hands in his pockets.

"You did?" said Rachel, looking surprised.

"Yes," replied Harold. "I was taking some photos of the lake earlier, behind your cabin. I also met your lovely daughter, Chloe. By the way, kiddo, did you find any more nice rocks?"

"Yes," Chloe replied. "A couple."

"That's good, perfect timing," Harold replied, looking up at the sky. "If you would have waited any longer, you'd be battling this snow to look for them."

Chloe grinned. "I don't mind. I love the snow. In fact, Mommy said we might go tubing this weekend."

He looked at Rachel. "That sounds like fun. By the way, I haven't formally introduced myself. I'm Harold," he said, holding out his hand. "It's nice to meet you."

"I'm Rachel," she replied, shaking it. "Nice to meet you, too."

The photographer looked at Mackenzie. "I'd better get started. If you don't mind, I'm going to just start taking pictures of the wedding party. Let me know if there is anything specific you'd like photographed."

"I want *everything* and *everybody*, so just start clicking away," she said, grinning.

He nodded. "Sounds great. Before I forget, I'd better go and find your mother, too. She had some suggestions she wanted to talk to me about."

"I'm sure she does. The woman is obsessed with making this weekend perfect and is already stressing out about the snow," replied Mackenzie. "Even more-so than me."

"You know, sometimes not having the perfect wedding makes it more memorable," said Harold with a wink, before walking away.

"Smart man," said Brock. "That's why I'm taking everything in stride."

"I wish I could. This weather is even making our minister late. He's not here yet," explained Mackenzie, glancing toward the doorway again.

"I'm sure the roads are starting to get pretty bad," said Brock. "And of course, people seem to forget how to drive in the snow, making everything worse. Hopefully, he didn't get stuck somewhere."

"What great timing, huh?" said Paul, frowning. "A blizzard on your wedding."

"I know," replied Mackenzie. "I'm just grateful that almost everyone arrived before the snow began. It would have been a rough ride from the cities."

"Apparently, it's not letting up anytime soon. If you're thinking about bolting, Brock, you'd better do it before you're snowed in," joked Paul.

"I can't. She took my keys. My wallet. My driver's license. And… my ability to be funny, apparently. I'm sorry, honey," he said, smiling sheepishly at Mackenzie, who was pretending to glare at him. "You know that first and foremost, you took my heart and I would *never* run out on you."

"Good answer," she said, now looking amused more than anything.

"Where would Brock run to, Mommy?" asked Chloe, who was watching them quietly.

"They're just kidding around," said Rachel, smiling down at her daughter. "Men do that when they're about to do something adultish and are anxious about it. That's why your dad is always joking around."

"Whoa," said Paul. "And on that note," he put his arm around Brock's shoulders, "as long as the minister is late, why don't we get ourselves a couple of stiff drinks, Brock? Something to keep us warm?"

"Sounds good. Do either of you want anything?" Brock asked the two women.

"No, thank you," said Rachel.

"I'm fine," said Mackenzie.

"What about you?" Brock asked Chloe. "I believe I saw some hot apple cider floating around here. I could get you a cup."

"I'm okay," she said.

"All-righty then. We'll be back shortly," said Brock, as Paul led him away.

"Don't take too long. The minister should be here any minute," called Mackenzie.

"I'm sorry. Paul's a bad influence," said Rachel with a sigh. "I'm sure he'll buy Brock a couple of shots, too."

"It's okay. Besides, Brock's a big boy and is responsible for any and all of his own bad choices," she replied, smiling.

"Are stiff drinks bad choices?" asked Chloe.

"You are *too* smart for your own good," said Mackenzie, leaning down. "You obviously take after your mother."

Rachel smiled.

"By the way, Chloe, Angie has been looking for you." She pointed toward Brock's niece, who was the same age. They'd played together a few times before and got along nicely. "See, she's over there, by her brother. Why don't you go and say hello?"

Her eyes lit up. "Okay!" she replied and then bolted away.

"So, how are things with you?" asked Mackenzie, when Chloe was out of ear-shot.

"Fine," replied Rachel, knowing what she was really asking. It wasn't a secret that Rachel and Paul were having problems. All they did was bicker about everything, especially lately. And that was when he was home. Lately, he'd been putting a lot of overtime at the advertising firm, where he worked.

"You know what you need? A romantic getaway. Just the two of you. I told you before that you can leave Chloe with me and Brock. Or, Maddy would even watch her."

"I don't know…"

"Seriously, Rachel. It would do you both good. When was the last time you two did anything by yourselves?"

Rachel gave her the same excuse as she always did. "It's been hard because Chloe is so young and, to be honest, I don't know if I could stand to be away from her for more than a couple of days. I work so much now as it is myself, and she's always with a sitter it seems."

"You're a worry-wort," she replied. "A few days away from Chloe won't hurt and it will do you and Paul some good."

"Maybe. I'll think about it. Thank you."

"No problem, now…" Mackenzie looked around the busy courtyard. "I saw you walk in with my sister. Do you know where she disappeared to?"

"No. Sorry."

"I wish she'd meet someone nice," said Mackenzie. "Brock has a big family. Maybe she will at the wedding."

"Why are you trying to set her up?" asked Rachel, surprised. "She's so young and has her life ahead of her. Besides, she's beautiful. She'll find someone."

"Unfortunately, she already has," said Mackenzie. She lowered her voice. "And, I think the guy is married or living with another woman."

Rachel's eyes widened. "Really? Have you met him?"

"No. In fact, I just heard about this guy last weekend. After the bachelorette party, she stayed overnight at my place and talked a little about him."

"What did she tell you?"

"Not much. I guess his name is John and they've been seeing each other for a few months. The bad part is... he's involved with someone, but trying to break it off."

She frowned. "Oh, no. That's not good."

"I know. But, she claims that she's falling in love with the guy and wants to wait to see what happens between him and his significant other."

"Is he married?"

"She wouldn't say. I'm sure she doesn't want me to give her the third-degree if he is. Anyway, I think she's going to get hurt and whoever this guy is, might just be stringing her along."

"You're probably right," Rachel replied, feeling sick to her stomach knowing that Maddy might indeed get hurt. She'd known her since she was a little girl and felt protective of her. "How did they even meet?"

"She was pretty vague about that, too." She forced a smile to her face. "Great. Here comes my mother. Don't say anything to her about it. She'll get upset."

"I won't." Rachel looked over to see Mackenzie's mother walk toward them. Carol was tall, thin, and as usual, impeccably dressed. Even though her shortly cropped hair had long ago turned white, she looked young for her age, which was somewhere in her late fifties. "Hi."

"Hello, Rachel," Carol said, smiling warmly. She pulled her into her arms for a hug. "It's been so long. How've you been?"

"Great," replied Rachel as she was released. "And you?"

"Stressed out, because of this damn snow," she replied, frowning. "And the minister still hasn't shown yet. Good grief, what's next?"

"It's not *that* bad, Mother," said Mackenzie. "It's actually very beautiful."

Rachel had to agree. It was like a winter wonderland around them. Especially with the glistening snow and twinkling white and red lights that were strewn around the courtyard. Plus, the staff were now handing out Styrofoam cups filled with apple cider.

"You know me, I'm not much of a snow person," replied Carol, shoving her hands into her coat pockets. "As long as you're happy, then that's all that matters."

"I'll be happier when we know that everyone is here safely," said Mackenzie.

"Me, too. By the way, where is Chloe?" asked Carol, looking around.

"She was with Angie, the last time I checked," replied Rachel, looking over to where she'd seen them last. Unfortunately, the girls were nowhere to be found.

"Great. I'd better go and look for them," said Rachel.

"And I suppose that I'd better go and see how everyone else is doing," said Mackenzie, smiling as another couple headed toward her. "Hi, Aunt Betty. Hi, Uncle Ted! I'm so glad you made it."

"I'll be back," Rachel told Carol.

"If I see her, I'll let you know," she answered.

"Thanks."

Chapter 12

CHLOE AND ANGIE were standing outside of the indoor pool area, staring longingly toward the water through the glass.

"I wish we could go swimming right now," said Angie, pressing her forehead against the pane as they watched two older kids play Marco Polo.

"I know. I brought my swimming suit. Did you?"

"Yes, but Mommy said that I can't go swimming until Sunday," replied Angie, frowning. "I have to wait until after the wedding."

"I'm going to ask if I can go after the rehearsal. I bet my mother will let me swim," said Chloe, who loved to swim. She'd been taking lessons since she was three years old and could go into the deep-end, as long as her mother was nearby, in case she needed her.

"You're lucky."

"Maybe your mom will change her mind and let you go swimming, too," said Chloe. "Especially if she finds out that my mom might watch you."

"Should we ask them?" asked Angie, smiling.

"Yes," said Chloe. "Let's go."

The two girls headed back the way they came. As they were about to step outside and into the courtyard, Rachel found them.

"Where have you been?" she asked sharply.

"We went to go look at the swimming pool," said Chloe. "You should see it! They have a whirlpool and a bunch of floaty toys to play with."

"Don't you ever take off like that again. You girls can't just go wandering around the lodge," Rachel said.

Chloe's eyes widened. "Angie just wanted to show me where the swimming pool was."

Angie swallowed. "Sorry."

Rachel sighed. "It's fine. Where did your brother go?" Angie's brother was twelve and usually watching over his younger sister, who was almost as precarious as Chloe.

"I don't know. I think he's playing with one of our cousins," said Angie.

"You'd better go and find your mother. She was worried about you, too," said Rachel.

"Okay," said Angie, going back out to the courtyard.

"Mommy, can you take us swimming later tonight?" asked Chloe.

"No," she replied. "Zip your jacket up before we go back outside."

"But, I want to go swimming and you said we could go earlier today, but never took me," said Chloe, stubbornly.

"I know. I'm sorry. Maybe tomorrow," replied Rachel.

Chloe groaned. "But, the wedding's tomorrow and you said there wouldn't be enough time. That's why you were going to take me today."

"We'll go Sunday or Monday," said Rachel, rubbing her temples.

"Hey, young ladies. No fighting," joked Brock.

They turned around to find him, Paul, and Maddy walking toward them in the hallway. All three were carrying cocktails and smiling.

"I want to go swimming later, but Mommy won't let me," said Chloe.

"There's no time tonight, sweetheart," said Paul. "After the rehearsal and dinner, it will be too late to do anything but go to bed."

"But, I don't want to go to the dinner," pouted Chloe. "It's going to be sooo... boring."

"My, my. Someone is definitely getting tired already," said Paul, bending down. "Should we bring you back to the cabin and put you to bed now since diner is too 'boring'?"

Chloe scowled.

"She has to stay for the rehearsal," said Rachel.

"Why? She's not the flower girl or the maid of honor. She's definitely not a groomsman. She really doesn't have to be here," he replied, as they all walked back outside into the courtyard.

"Heck, at this rate, I don't have to either," said Brock, looking at his watch. "It looks like the minister hasn't even made it here yet."

"Exactly. We could be waiting around all night," said Paul, taking a drink of his cocktail.

"Still, she needs to eat. I'm sure dinner will be soon, even if we have to wait on the rehearsal," said Rachel.

"Dinner is supposed to be at eight. You know, once she eats, I can bring her back to my cabin. Then you can relax and spend some time with Mackenzie. I know she was looking forward to seeing you," said Maddy.

"Aren't you in the wedding?" asked Paul.

"No. I have this weird phobia about standing in front of a large group of people and having them stare at me," she replied, looking embarrassed. "It makes me almost... hyperventilate, I get so anxious. It's stupid, I know..."

"It's not stupid," said Rachel, smiling at her. "I've always hated speaking to large groups of people myself. I feel like throwing up most of the time. Even now, at twenty-nine years old, I'm still nervous about it."

"What is it that you do again?" asked Brock.

"I'm a computer analyst. Sometimes I help train new staff for the company I work for," said Rachel. "And that's when my anxiety begins to show."

"You always seem so confident about everything," said Maddy.

"It's all a façade," she replied, winking.

"Don't let her fool you. Nothing seems to scare Rachel. Sometimes I think her balls are bigger than mine."

Rachel frowned. She could tell that Paul was already tipsy, which made her uncomfortable. He tended to get mouthy and almost always embarrassed her.

"Hey, there's the minister," said Brock, as an older gentleman stepped into the courtyard with an apologetic smile.

"Yes, here I am," said the man, walking over to him. He held out his hand. "I'm so sorry I'm late. The roads are atrocious."

"No problem at all. I'm just glad you made it here safely," said Brock, shaking the minister's hand. "By the way, Pastor Bill, these are friends of ours. Paul, Rachel, and Chloe. Obviously, you already know Maddy."

"Yes," he replied, smiling at them warmly. "Nice meeting you. Well, shall we get this rehearsal started, Brock? I'm sure everyone wants to get back inside, where it's warmer."

"Yes, indeed. Let's go find Mackenzie," he replied.

"I'd rather be swimming," mumbled Chloe.

"Don't worry," said Maddy, leaning down next to her. "You and I will have fun back at my cabin. We'll watch a movie or something. After dinner, of course."

Chloe smiled in relief. "Okay."

Chapter 13

"HOLD UP, NOW," said Alex. "Carissa is *not* responsible for this."

"Then how in the hell did she know all of that shit?" he asked angrily.

"I'm a clairvoyant," said Carissa.

Jim's head whipped back to her. "What? You've got to be kidding me?" he muttered.

"I realize that you don't believe me," said Carissa. "But, you've got to let me help with this case. If we don't find him, he'll do it again. And soon."

"I'm sorry, but I don't believe in that ridiculous, psychic crap," he replied.

Carissa knew she had to do something quickly, or she'd either be arrested or at the very least, made to leave. "Give me your hand. I'll prove that I can help you."

"Lady, this isn't some kind of game. I don't have time for this. I'm sorry, but it looks like I'm going to have to arrest you," he said, taking out his handcuffs.

"Please. Just humor me and if I don't change your mind, I'll go with you peacefully," she replied.

Jim looked at Alex and shook his head.

"Just give her a few seconds, Jim," said Alex. "I think you're going to be glad you did."

He swore. "Fine. For you, I will. But, that's only because we've been friends for a long time and I trust you. I also know how you're not one to believe in this psychic mumbo-jumbo stuff." He grunted. "To be honest, I'm curious to find out what she's going to say next."

Alex relaxed. "Carissa is not a killer. And… she knew things about me that she shouldn't have," Alex said. "Just like she knew about the little girl you found earlier."

The sheriff, still looking a little perturbed, allowed Carissa to take his hand.

She closed her eyes and tried focusing on him this time. The visions came quickly.

"You've been married for a very long time and… your wife is ill," she said, frowning.

"She has cancer," he replied grimly.

"Your daughter doesn't know, does she?" said Carissa. "She's in college. Texas University?"

Jim stiffened up. "Yeah."

"Your wife doesn't want her to know. She's afraid she'll drop her studies and come back to care for her. Her name is… Jen? Or… Gwen? No, it's…" She opened her eyes. "It's Jacqueline. Your daughter's name is Jacqueline."

Stunned, Jim pulled his hand away. "Yes."

"Your wife needs to tell her. She deserves to know," said Carissa.

Jim looked at her and then at Alex. "Did you tell her about Jacqueline?"

"No. Of course not," he replied. "I didn't even know your wife had cancer."

Jim looked at Carissa again. "That's indeed some crazy shit. I don't know what to believe."

"I'm not a killer," said Carissa, staring at him hard. "If I was, do you really think I'd come back here and offer to help you solve the murder?"

"Sometimes the perps come back to gloat," he grumbled. "Or throw us off-course."

It was then that it hit her. "That's what he was doing," she said, thinking about the dead girl again. "He wants you to think he's a child molester but… he isn't. He's trying to confuse you."

"The only one confusing me right now is you," said the sheriff, looking haggard. "I really do need to have you come down to the station so we can talk more about this."

"There's no time," she said. "He's going to strike again. He's looking for his daughter."

Jim's eyes widened. "His daughter?"

She nodded quickly. "Yes. He's delirious and wants her back. When he realizes that the child isn't his little girl, he gets rid of her."

"Good God," said Alex, looking ill.

"So, you think this is the work of some distraught father?" asked the sheriff, not looking convinced.

"Yes. Distraught and mentally ill, obviously," she said.

86

"Ma'am, I really do wish I could believe what you're telling me and run with it. It would make my job so much easier. But there is no way in hell I can trust a couple of hunches, even if you do have some kind of… psychic gift."

"I understand and, believe me, I'm used to not being taken seriously. But what if I'm right about everything and another girl dies?" she replied.

Jim let out a ragged sigh. "So, what is it that you want to do?"

"I need to see her body." As sad as it would be, she knew that it would give her more insight and possibly save another one.

"Fine. You can see her at the coroner's facility," he replied. "In fact, it looks like they are done with her and she'll be heading there, soon."

Carissa looked over and saw that the little girl was being placed in a body bag. Seeing that made her heart bleed. She couldn't let this happen again. Not if she could do something about it.

"Let me see her *now*," begged Carissa. "I don't know if I'll learn anything new, but I have to try."

"Come on, Jim. She just told you things that she shouldn't have known anything about. Give her a chance," said Alex.

Jim ran a hand over his face. "Jesus."

"I just need a few seconds," said Carissa. "That's it."

"Fine," he replied sharply. "But, I'm still bringing you in for questioning, young lady."

She sighed in relief. "Of course and I'll answer whatever you want."

"Wait here," he said and then trudged through the snow to the forensic team.

Shivering from the cold, Carissa looked over at Alex. He was staring at her quietly.

"Thank you," she said.

He smiled grimly. "I'm starting to think that we'll be the ones thanking you."

"I hope so," she said softly.

Chapter 14

AFTER REHEARSAL, THE wedding party went into Blue
Waters, to an area that had been sectioned off for them for dinner.

"Mommy, I have to go to the bathroom," said Chloe, a few
minutes after they were seated.

"I can take her, if you'd like. I'd like to wash my hands
anyway," volunteered Maddy.

"Would you? Thanks so much," said Rachel, smiling in relief.
Mackenzie had just poured her a glass of wine and they'd been
reminiscing about their days in college.

"No problem. Let's go," said Maddy. "Come on, kiddo."

The two stood up and headed toward the bathrooms, when
they ran into Harold.

"Hello, again," he said, smiling brightly.

"Hi, Harold," said Maddy. "Busy, night, huh?"

"Not too bad. Your mother definitely has me running with the
camera," he replied, looking amused. "But, that's why I'm here. To
make sure your sister has some great shots of today and
tomorrow."

"My mother is *very* demanding" she said. "Speaking of being here, where's your fiancée?"

"Oh, she stayed home," he replied. "It's been a long week for her and she just wanted to kick up her feet and relax."

"Is she also a photographer?" Maddy asked.

"No. She's a librarian. Anyway, she might come tomorrow."

"Good. I look forward to meeting her," she replied.

"Maddy, I've gotta go potty really, *really* badly," whined Chloe, shuffling from one foot to the other.

"Sorry, kiddo. See you later, Harold," she said, pushing open the bathroom door.

"Most definitely."

"Are you almost finished?" asked Maddy, five minutes later. From experience, she knew that it sometimes took the little girl a long time to do her business.

"Yes."

Maddy glanced at her reflection in the mirror and pushed a strand of hair back into place. She then applied some lipstick and rubbed her lips together. As she put the tube back into her purse, Chloe began to sing *Rudolph the Red Nosed Reindeer*.

"Hey, kiddo? I'm going to wait outside for you."

"Don't leave me!"

"Relax. I'll just be in the hallway. I want to make a phone call anyway."

Chloe sighed. "Okay."

Maddy stepped outside of the bathroom, almost bumping into one of the hotel staff, a good-looking guy with blond hair, bright blue eyes, and thick eyebrows. He was holding two large rolls of brown paper towels.

"I'm so sorry," Maddy said. "I almost ran you over."

"No, it's my fault. I was in a hurry and not paying attention," he replied, smiling. "By the way, someone mentioned that they were out of paper towels in the women's room? Is that right?"

"I used the hand dryer, so I'm really not sure," she said as her phone began to buzz.

"Is there anyone else inside?" he asked, watching as she pulled out her cell phone.

"Just my friend's little girl. She should almost be done."

"Okay," he replied, leaning against the back wall. "I can wait."

While Maddy sent a text, she felt the guy's eyes on her. She had to admit – he was cute. Very cute. But she wasn't interested. Maddy was in love with a man who took her breath away. The only problem was that he was married and taking his sweet time in leaving his wife. But he'd sworn to Maddy that his heart belonged to her and very soon, they'd be together.

Her cell phone buzzed with a text from him. Butterflies swarmed in her stomach as she quickly read the message:

It's not a good time.

Maddy sighed and texted him back:

Are you going to tell her this weekend?

He replied that he would try but wanted to wait until it was the right time.

Gritting her teeth, she put her phone away.

"So, are you with the wedding party?" asked the stranger.

Maddy looked up. "Yes. My sister is actually the bride-to-be."

"Ah. You two look alike. My name is Ben, by the way."

"I'm Maddy," she replied, noticing that he had a dazzling white smile. He reminded her of someone from a toothpaste commercial.

"I usually bartend, but we're short on staff tonight."

"And that's how you got stuck with toilet duties?" she teased.

He chuckled. "Yeah. I only do paper towel and soap refills, though. I draw the line at anything else."

"I don't blame you."

Smiling again, he yawned.

"Long day?" she asked.

He nodded. "It's going to be an even longer night. I don't mind, though. I have nothing else going on or anybody waiting for me at home."

She bit back a smile. That was subtle. "Lucky you."

"I don't know about luck. It gets pretty lonely, especially on cold winter nights," he said with a flirtatious smile. "I'm hoping that might change soon."

He was definitely a player. Although she wasn't interested, she could tell he liked her and if felt good to be appreciated. "I like your optimism. Hopefully it will pay off."

Before he could respond, the door opened and Chloe walked out.

"Did you wash your hands?" asked Maddy.

Chloe nodded and held them up. "But there weren't any paper towels, so I had to wipe my hands on my pants."

"You could have used the dryer," replied Maddy.

"I don't like the kind they have. It's too loud," she replied.

"You have a point. The high velocity dryers are definitely loud," said Ben. "I'm going to go and refill the dispensers. Do you want some?"

"No. I'm okay," she replied, wiping them on her pants again.

Maddy grabbed her hand. "We'd better go back to the table before your mother begins to worry. See you around, Ben."

"I hope so," he said, giving her another disarming smile.

"Who was that?" asked Chloe, glancing at him over her shoulder as Maddy pulled her down the hallway. He was still watching them. He winked at Chloe and she smiled.

"Someone who works here," she replied.

"He's handsome."

Maddy smiled. "You noticed it too, huh?"

"Yes. Not as good looking as my daddy, though," she replied. "Nobody is as good looking as he is."

Maddy chuckled. "You love your daddy very much, don't you?"

She nodded. "I just wish…"

"What?"

"That he would play with me more. He used to. Now all he cares about is his stupid phone. He loves it more than he loves me," she pouted.

Maddy stopped and bent down on one knee. "Honey, your daddy loves you very much," she said, brushing the hair out of Chloe's eyes. "Don't you ever think otherwise."

Chloe didn't reply.

She sighed. "Do you want me to talk to him?"

Chloe's eyes widened. "No. He'll get mad."

"Not if he knows how upset you are," said Maddy. "I think he'd want to know how you really feel."

"But I tell him all the time and he ignores me."

Maddy knew that Paul could sometimes be an ass, but he loved Chloe and would want to know about their conversation. "I'll talk to him."

She sucked in her breath. "But–"

"Don't worry. I'll do it in a way that will not make him angry with you, okay?"

"Okay," said Chloe, smiling in relief. If there was one person she trusted, it was Maddy.

Chapter 15

AFTER SPEAKING TO the Forensics team, the sheriff walked back over to them.

"Okay. You have a couple of minutes, but that's it," he said. "We need to wrap this up."

"Thank you," she replied.

They followed Jim over to the girl's body. The investigators had zipped up the bag and the sheriff knelt down to reopen it. "I'm only doing this because I don't want anyone to ever say that I didn't go down every avenue to find this lunatic."

"He'll be caught," she said firmly.

He looked over his shoulder at her. "That's one thing you and I can agree on. I will find this bastard and make him pay for what he did to this sweet little girl."

She nodded.

He unzipped the bag, exposing the little girl's face and Carissa immediately had to blink back tears.

Pale, porcelain-like skin, long, blonde lashes, and bowtie lips that had smiled for most of her young life.

"She'd been a happy little girl," whispered Carissa, reaching out to touch her cold forehead.

"No. You're not allowed to tamper with the body. Nobody touches her without gloves," said Jim.

She pulled her hand back. "As much as I don't want to disturb her, I have to do it this way."

He looked over at the other investigators, who were watching from a distance. "Jesus. Fine. Do it." Jim looked at Alex. "Block their view. If they see her do it, I'll have to explain why and I'm not in the mood for that right now."

He did as Jim asked. "How long has she been dead, Jim? Do they have any idea?" Alex asked, staring down at the girl.

"Since last night," Carissa answered for him.

Jim nodded. "Yeah."

Although the child's spirit was gone, Carissa still picked up fragments of energy and it made her throat tighten.

Please don't hurt me...

She'd begged for her life, out here in the cold. There'd been a small chase, and then he'd strangled her. Knowing the kind of terror the child had gone through before dying, Carissa almost lost it.

As if reading her mind, Alex looked away in disgust. "How could anyone do this? Sick bastard."

Taking a deep breath, Carissa closed her eyes and concentrated. After several seconds, more things came to her.

The man picked them up after a soccer game. There'd been two little girls, but he'd let one go.

"Are you getting anything?" asked the sheriff, getting impatient.

"Yes. Please, let me concentrate," she said, not opening her eyes.

He sighed. "Sorry."

More images were shown to her. The child had spent several days in the man's basement, terrified. He'd tried giving her things to make her happy.

Stuffed animals.

Toys.

A dog.

She clenched her jaw. The bastard had used the puppy as bait.

You're not Faith…

She opened her eyes.

"I think her name was Annie or Amy," she said, removing her hand from the girl's forehead. "She played soccer. He picked her up after a game. There was another girl with her, too. But surprisingly, he let the other one go."

Alex and Jim looked at each other.

She stood up and brushed the snow off of her jeans. "He had a puppy. He used it to draw out the girls."

"What else?" asked Alex.

"He's passionate about soccer. In fact, that's how he found her." Staring into the distance she chewed on her lip. "I'm not sure but… I think he's much older. He walks with a cane and there was something about arthritis that I was picking up."

"I'll be damned," said Jim, pulling out a pen and paper. "You didn't happen to get the perp's name address, or social security number, did you?"

"I wish it were that easy," she replied, staring down at the girl, who looked so peaceful. It seemed so out of place, considering how violent her death had been.

"Is there anything else you can tell me?" asked the sheriff.

Pleased that Jim wasn't brushing off her ramblings, she nodded. "I know the name of his daughter. It's Faith. He'll keep searching for her until we catch him."

Alex stared at her in surprise. "Faith?"

"Yes. Does that mean anything to you?" she asked him.

"No. Are you sure that 'Faith' is not just some kind of metaphor that your visions are picking up on?" asked Alex.

"Yeah, maybe the guy is on some kind of zealous religious quest," added Jim.

"He's on a quest, but religion has nothing to do with it," she said grimly.

Chapter 16

AFTER DINNER, CHLOE reminded Maddy of her promise to take her back to her cabin.

"Sure," she replied. "As long as your parents are okay with it."

"Are you sure it's not a bother?" asked Rachel.

"Not at all," she replied. "Chloe and I can watch a movie."

"Yay!" cried Chloe. "Can I stay the night with you?"

"If you want," she replied.

"Are you sure?" asked Rachel.

"Yes. It's kind of lonely there anyway, since I rented it all by myself," said Maddy. She patted Chloe's hand. "You can keep me company."

"I will. Can we go and get my blanket and pajamas?" she asked.

"Of course," replied Maddy.

"Chloe, you'd better be on your best behavior and do whatever she tells you to do," said Rachel, still looking a little uncertain.

"I will. I promise," said Chloe, crossing her heart.

"Are you sure you want her *all* night?" Paul asked, leaning back in the chair.

"Yes. Besides, she's always a good girl when she's with me," said Maddy. "And, it's not like I have anything else going on."

"Thanks, Maddy," said Mackenzie, who'd been listening in. "I told Rachel that she needed to let loose and have some fun this weekend. Including tonight. I heard they're going to have karaoke in the bar area, soon."

"Oh no," groaned Rachel.

"Oh yes," said Mackenzie, smiling. "You're getting up there and singing."

"Mommy is going to sing?" asked Chloe, looking intrigued.

"No, Mommy is not," said Rachel dryly.

"Yes, she is," replied Mackenzie. "I'll get her up there. Have you ever heard her sing?"

"Sometimes, but not karaoke," said Chloe.

"I'm not going to sing," argued Rachel.

Mackenzie winked at Chloe. "That's what she thinks."

***

Fifteen minutes later, everyone was in the main bar area, including Chloe and Maddy.

"Just one song," begged Mackenzie. "Think of it as a wedding gift. To your very best friend in the world."

"Guilt trip. Thanks. Why do you want me to do this so badly?" she asked, staring at her friend.

"Because you have a beautiful voice. You should have been a singer. Haven't I always told you that?"

You know how I hate this," she said, looking around the crowded bar. There were a lot of people there, even with the bad weather. Many were family and friends of Brock's and Mackenzie's, but there were some locals, too. "I was just telling Maddy earlier how much I hate talking in front of large groups, and now I'll be singing?"

"Here," said Brock, handing her and Mackenzie a shot of something red.

"What's this?" asked Rachel, looking down.

"A raspberry Kamikaze," she replied. "I had Brock get us both one. I know how much you used to love Kamis."

Rachel smiled. "They are good."

"I'm sorry, would you like one, too, Maddy?" asked Brock.

"No. I'm leaving soon with Chloe. After Rachel sings," she replied. "But, thanks."

"By the way, Maddy – that bartender keeps checking you out," said Rachel.

Maddy turned around and saw Ben, who was back at his station. Their eyes met and he winked at her.

She smiled.

"He's cute. You should go and talk to him," said Mackenzie.

"I did. Earlier," replied Maddy and then explained how she'd seen him by the bathrooms.

"Bartenders are bad news," said Paul. "They're players. Not exactly what Maddy needs."

"What's a player?" asked Chloe, her eyes wide.

"Someone who isn't to be trusted," he replied.

"Why?"

"For many reasons. You know, I think your mommy should hurry up and sing a song so you can leave with Maddy. It's getting way past your bedtime," said Paul, ruffling up her hair.

"But, I don't want to go to bed," said Chloe, smoothing it back down.

"It is getting pretty late. Rachel, you'd better drink that shot and pick a song," said Brock.

"Oh, fine." Rachel chugged the sweet liquor and shuddered in delight. "Wow, I forgot how good those were."

"Can I have one?" asked Chloe, staring at the empty glass.

"No. It's a grownup drink," said Rachel, feeling her stomach get warm. "So, what song shall I sing?"

"Can I pick it out?" asked Chloe.

"Of course," said Rachel. "Let's go and see what they have."

Five minutes later, Rachel was on stage and singing the words to the song, "For Your Eyes Only."

"She definitely has no reason to be afraid of crowds," said Maddy. "Not with a voice like that."

"Without the Kamikaze, she wouldn't have gotten out there. She really is self-conscious," said Paul, watching his wife. "But, I have to admit – she does have an amazing voice."

"Wow," said Chloe. "I didn't know Mommy could sing like that."

"Neither did I," said Paul, folding his arms across his chest. His eyes met Rachel's and he smiled at her.

"Didn't I tell you?" said Mackenzie, elbowing Brock. "She could have been a singer."

"She's very good," he agreed. "You should have asked her to sing at our wedding."

"I don't think there's enough booze in the bar to give her that kind of courage," joked Mackenzie.

When the song was finished, the bar erupted in applause; even the bartenders clapped.

Rachel set the mic down and hurried off the stage.

"You were amazing," said Mackenzie, putting an arm around her. She kissed her cheek. "Thanks for the present."

Rachel blushed.

"Mommy, you were *so* awesome!" cried Chloe, throwing her arms around her mother's waist.

"Thank you, sweetheart," said Rachel, kissing the top of her head. "I'm glad you liked it."

"Wasn't she great, Daddy?" Chloe said, turning to look at her father.

"Yes. Very. I had no idea you could sing that well," said Paul, grinning. He pulled her into his arms and hugged her.

"How about another song?" said Chloe.

"Chloe, it's getting late. We should probably get going," said Maddy.

"But I want to hear her Mommy sing again," she replied.

"Sorry, but that was it for me," said Rachel. She bent down and gave Chloe a kiss on the nose. "Now, you be good for Maddy, okay?"

Chloe sighed. "I will."

"It's pretty late. I'd better walk you two ladies back to the cabin so you can grab Chloe's overnight things," said Paul, finishing up his drink.

"That would be great," said Maddy, putting on her coat.

Rachel helped Chloe get her jacket on and then hugged and kissed her. "I love you, sweetie."

"I love you, too, Mommy," she replied.

Rachel let her go and then Chloe gave Mackenzie a hug.

"I'll be back," Paul said, grabbing his jacket from the back of his chair.

Rachel watched the three of them walk out, and for a second, she wanted to leave, too.

"She's a great kid," said Mackenzie, popping a green olive into her mouth.

"Yes, she certainly is," said Rachel, smiling. "I don't know what I'd do without her."

***

Chloe followed closely behind Paul and Maddy as they took the path to her parents' cabin. Fortunately, management had someone with a snow-blower already clearing the walkways.

"Can we make a snowman?" asked Chloe.

"Not tonight," replied Maddy, glancing back at her. "Besides, the snow is too soft and won't stick."

"What do you mean?" asked Paul, picking up a handful of the white powder. He packed it into his gloved hand and threw it at Maddy's face.

"Paul!" she squealed.

"Okay, maybe it's a little too soft," he replied, trying to pick up more snow.

Maddy quickly leaned down and grabbed a handful herself. Soon all three of them were laughing and throwing snow at each other.

"Okay. Enough." Paul smiled as he shook the snow out of his hair. "Two against one. I see how you ladies operate."

"Your fault. You started it. Anyway, we'd better hurry," said Maddy, her cheeks flushed from the cold. "Rachel will start wondering what's taking so long."

He grabbed Chloe's hand. "Are you cold?"

"No," she replied, staring up at him as they began walking again. "That was fun."

"It *was* fun," he agreed, winking at her.

"Can you help me build a snowman tomorrow, Daddy?" she asked.

"Maybe. We'll see if the snow is stickier," he said, smiling down at her.

It wasn't a 'no' and it gave Chloe hope. "We haven't made one together in a long time. Usually Mommy makes a snowman with me."

He was quiet for a few seconds. "Tell you what – the next one will be made by just you and me. And it will be the biggest, baddest snowman you've ever seen."

"Yes!" cried Chloe. "Can we put a hat and scarf on it, too?"

"Of course," he replied. "Whatever you want, honey."

"I love you, Daddy," she said, snuggling up against him.

"I love you, too." He picked Chloe up and put her over his shoulders, making her giggle in pleasure.

When they finally reached the cabin, Chloe ran to her bedroom to grab her things to take to Maddy's. When she had what she needed, she ran back to the living area, but didn't see Maddy or her father. Hearing laughter coming from her parents' bedroom, she skipped down the hallway and looked inside to see what was so funny. What she saw confused her: her daddy and Maddy were kissing. And it wasn't how friends kissed.

Frozen in shock, she just stared at them until Maddy noticed her.

"Oh, my God. Chloe," she said, pushing Paul away. Her face was bright red. "We didn't hear you."

"Why were you kissing my daddy?" Chloe asked angrily.

Maddy looked at Paul helplessly. "See, you should have told her last week."

"Told me what?" asked Chloe, her eyes filling with tears. Something was very wrong.

"Nothing. Look, sweetie, it was just a friendly kiss," said Paul, getting down on his knee in front of her. "That's all."

"You had your hands on her private area," she said, backing away from him.

"If I did, it was an accident," said Paul, trying to reach for her. "But I think you were seeing things."

"No, I wasn't!" cried Chloe, pushing him away. What she'd seen didn't look at all like an accident. Both he and Maddy had betrayed her mother and the painful realization made her cry even harder. "I want my mommy!"

"Chloe. Relax," said Paul, trying to calm her.

She turned around, ran out of the room, and then out of the cabin to find her mother. As she raced down the path back toward the lodge, she could hear her dad calling for her.

Ignoring him, she continued running until she slipped and fell on the ice.

"Honey, are you okay?"

Sobbing, she looked up to see Harold staring down at her with concern.

Chapter 17

WHEN ALL WAS said and done, the sheriff changed his mind about having her return with him to the station.

"Obviously you weren't a witness and I don't believe that you're responsible for this child's death. I would like to see your I.D. and get your phone number, however, in case I have any questions," Jim said.

"Okay," she replied, reaching into her purse. She handed him her driver's license and he walked over to his squad car with it.

"Hopefully, they'll I.D. the body soon," said Alex. "You said she's from Duluth?"

"I believe so. I'm sure the sheriff will learn pretty quickly who she is, especially since this guy let her friend go. Not many cases like that." Carissa thought about the murdered child's parents and knew it was going to be a devastating blow for them.

"So, the little girl in your dreams, the girl we looked at wasn't her?"

"No," she replied.

"Do you think he has your girl yet?"'

"I don't know. Hopefully not. He had Amy for a few days before he killed her, though. Something tells me that it was a struggle for him to murder the little girl after he realized she wasn't his daughter."

"Hm. Was there anything else that you picked up on?"

The fact that he was starting to accept that she really did have psychic abilities made her want to prove herself that much more.

"Actually, there was one more thing – I almost feel like Faith's mother may have run off with his daughter and that's why he's looking for her. *Been* looking for her."

"So, he's probably responsible for more than one dead child. I wonder how long he's been searching for his daughter."

"I don't know. I mean, it's possible that it's been years and if that's the case," she sighed, "then Faith could even be a grown woman by now."

He grunted. "Wouldn't that be something?"

"Yeah."

"I'm curious – how many cases have you helped solve?" Alex asked.

Carissa thought back. "Officially? About seven. There were a lot of others I tried helping with, but the police thought I was nuts and brushed me off."

"It is hard to absorb. You've convinced me, though."

Carissa smiled.

"So, how does this work? You have these dreams and then just pack up and go?"

"Pretty much."

"Do you ever get paid?"

"No. I don't expect to, either."

"How do you earn a living then?"

"Let's just say that I've made some good investment choices."

He stared at her in surprise. "Stocks and bonds? No lottery winnings or Vegas trips?"

She laughed. "No, I don't gamble."

"But, you've been able to benefit a little financially from your psychic gifts? That's good."

"Not really. To be honest, my grandmother left me some money when she died. I invested it, but my broker did all the work. I didn't use my abilities to choose the investments."

"So, you lucked out."

"Apparently." Although, Carissa had felt 'right' about choosing her broker, however, and assumed there was some kind divine intervention involved. She never had to worry about money, although she wasn't one to live above her means. She had twenty grand in her savings, her house was paid off, and every month she profited from her investments. Not a huge amount, but enough to keep her doing what she was doing.

"Let's just hope that your luck pans out this time as well and we can find this little girl from your dreams before the killer does."

Although she wanted to remain positive, something told her that she may already be too late.

Chapter 18

"HERE, LET ME help you up," said Harold, reaching for her.

Chloe let him pick her up off the ground. As he set her back down on her feet, he noticed her tears.

"Are you hurt?" he asked.

Wiping her tears with the back of her hand, she shook her head.

"Chloe, there you are," said Paul, rushing over to them. "Are you okay?"

She didn't say anything.

"She took a spill," explained Harold.

"Oh, honey," he said, pulling her into his arms. "You had me worried half to death. Don't ever take off like that, especially when it's dark out."

Chloe went rigid. She was still angry with him. "I want my mommy."

Paul released her. "Mommy's busy right now. Let's get you back to the cabin," he said softly.

"No. I don't want to go anywhere with you," she said, noticing that Maddy was now with them. Chloe glared at her.

"Sounds like someone is tired," said Harold. "Hopefully tomorrow will be a better day. Well, I'd best be off. Goodnight, folks."

"Goodnight," said Paul, grabbing Chloe's hand.

"Goodnight, Harold," said Maddy.

Paul began walking Chloe back toward the cabin.

"Should I come with?" asked Maddy.

"No," said Paul, not looking at her.

Chloe didn't say anything to her father and he was also quiet on the way back. When they arrived, Paul reached into his pocket for the keycard and swore. He'd left it inside on the counter.

"We need to go and get another key," he said, turning around. "Come on, Chloe."

She went with him silently.

As they headed back toward the lodge, Paul tried talking to her again. "I know you're angry and you think you saw something… but, you were mistaken, okay?"

She didn't reply.

"I love your mother and I love you," he said.

"Then why did you kiss Maddy?" she asked in a frightened voice.

"It was only a friendly kiss. You need to believe that."

Chloe didn't answer. She knew what she'd seen but wanted to believe her father. The idea that he would kiss Maddy the same way he would kiss her mother didn't make any sense.

"I think you just need a good night's sleep. There's been too much excitement today," he continued. "When you're exhausted, it can sometimes mess with your head."

Chloe didn't want to think or talk about it anymore. It made her feel anxious.

When they arrived back at the lodge, he brought her inside and told her to sit down and wait in the lounge, next to the fireplace.

"I'll be right back. I'm going to run into the bar and grab your mother's keycard."

"I want to come with," she said, needing to feel her mother's comforting arms around her.

"Honey, it will only take me a few seconds. Just, sit still and wait. Don't go anywhere."

"Fine," she mumbled.

"Go on. Sit down and wait for me," he said before disappearing down the hallway.

Chloe sank down into the sofa, looking up at the tall, stuffed grizzly bear next to the fireplace. Her mother had told her that it had once been alive. With its big, black claws and fierce expression, it scared her a little.

"Chloe," said a man's voice.

She turned her head and looked at him. Although he was wearing a hoodie and winter jacket, she recognized him but couldn't remember his name.

"It's time to go," he said, holding out his hand.

She frowned. "Go where?"

He leaned down and smiled. "Your dad said that you've been having a rough night and asked me to bring you back to the cabin. He said he'd return shortly. He's having a beer."

"A beer?" she asked, frowning. "He said he'd be right back."

"He changed his mind. He didn't want you sitting out here by yourself, so he sent me."

She hesitated.

"Come on," he said, still holding out his hand. "They'll be shutting off the lights here in a few seconds. You don't want to sit alone in the dark, waiting for him when you could be back at the cabin, watching television."

Looking up at the bear, she took his hand. She definitely didn't want to be in the dark with the scary animal staring down at her.

"Good girl," he said, smiling as Chloe stood up.

They stepped outside into the cold darkness and he began leading her toward the parking lot.

"Wait," Chloe said, stopping abruptly. She pointed. "My cabin is that way."

"I know," he replied. "We're taking my car over. I saw you slip and fall. I'd hate to have it happen again."

"Okay," she replied.

There was another parking lot in front of her parents' cabin. That's where her daddy had parked their truck. It would definitely be easier than walking all the way down the path.

When they reached his car, he opened up the back door and told her to get in.

Chloe suddenly felt funny about the situation. "Actually, I think we should just walk. I won't slip," she said, remembering how her mother had always told her to never get into a vehicle with anyone other than a family member. Unless… they used the password.

"Don't be silly. It will just take a few seconds to drive over there."

"Uh, did my daddy tell you the password?" she asked, feeling even more anxious.

He gave her a puzzled look. "For what?"

"To get into your car."

It took him a few seconds to answer. "No, but he thought that I was going to walk you to the cabin, so it never came up."

She chewed on her lower lip. It made sense, but she still felt like she was doing something wrong.

He leaned down and smiled at her. "You're not scared of me, are you? Am I really *that* ugly?" he joked.

"No," she said shyly. "But–"

"Chloe!" hollered her father.

Chloe turned around and saw him standing outside of the main lodge, looking around. Before she could answer, the man shoved a wet, smelly rag over her mouth and then everything went dark.

Chapter 19

HIS HEART RACED as he quickly placed the little girl into the backseat of the car, wishing he'd brought the van that morning. He covered her with a blanket and then stood back up to assess the situation.

Thankfully, Paul, who was too far away to notice what was happening, turned around and went back into the lodge.

Shaking with excitement, he quickly got into his vehicle and started the engine. He'd been so lucky. If she'd have given him any more hesitation, Paul would have arrived and things would have gotten ugly. But luck had been on his side and he'd gotten his daughter back.

He glanced back at Faith in the rearview mirror. "It's just you and me now, pumpkin. I have some things I need to do tomorrow, but then after that, we're leaving for good. I'm just so relieved that everything fell into place."

His timing couldn't have been better. He'd seen her leave with Paul and Maddy, and had followed them. Even at that point, he hadn't known exactly what he was going to do.

After watching them clown around in the snow for a while, they finally disappeared into the cabin. By then he was both frustrated and anxious. Deciding that he might have to take Faith back by force, he hurried over to his car and grabbed his gun. He didn't want to have to use it, but knew that desperate times sometimes called for desperate measures.

As he was about to race back to their cabin, he noticed Faith running away from it and then Harold intercepting her. She looked upset and it had made him that much more determined to get her back. A few seconds later, Paul arrived and he brought her back to the cabin. Instead of going inside, however, they turned around and left again. Confused, he waited a few seconds and then followed them into the lodge. Noticing Eva, the front desk clerk, was away from her post, and that Paul had left Faith alone, he quickly sprang into action. The rest was history.

He quickly drove out of the parking lot, aware that very soon, the police would be called and there'd be a hunt for her. They'd question everyone in the area, and eventually come knocking at his door. Although he was tempted to leave town right away, he wanted to withdraw the money from his accounts and the banks weren't open until morning. He wasn't too worried, however. Even if the cops showed up, they'd never suspect him of taking the girl. They'd just want to know if he'd seen anything unusual.

An idea suddenly came to him.

Harold.

In the morning, after he drained his savings, he'd use a payphone and leave an anonymous tip. He'd tell the police that he'd seen Harold with the girl and they'd focus their attention on the old man while he and Faith headed to Alaska.

He smiled. It was a brilliant idea.

Driving steadily on the slippery roads, it took him thirty minutes to reach the cabin. He pulled into the garage, closed the door, and carried Faith inside.

"Maisie. Guess who I brought home?" he said as the Beagle barked, excited to see him. "Faith. She's sleeping right now but don't worry, you can play with her tomorrow. You two are going to be best buddies."

Maisie barked again.

"I'm sure you're hungry. I'll let you out and feed you right after I put her to bed," he told the puppy as he headed toward the basement stairs with Faith still cradled in his arms.

Maisie followed him downstairs and into the bedroom.

He turned on the light, walked over to the bed, and carefully set Faith onto the mattress. He then removed her jacket and shoes.

"Sleep tight, pumpkin," he whispered, pulling the covers around her. "Tomorrow is a new beginning for both of us."

Kissing her forehead, he smiled and turned on the butterfly nightlight next to her bed. Then he walked out of the bedroom, turned off the light, and locked the door behind him.

Chapter 20

ALEX DROPPED CARISSA off at her SUV around eleven-thirty. The snow had finally stopped, although the roads were still slippery.

"Are you sure you don't want me to drive you back to the lodge?" he asked. "I'm sure they won't mind if you leave your vehicle here overnight."

"No. I'll be fine. Besides," she nodded toward a truck that was clearing snow on the other side of the parking lot, "I'm sure they want to plow right here."

"I suppose. I can follow you, if you'd like?"

Carissa appreciated his concern and thought that his ex-wife had been an idiot. "I'll be fine. Really."

"Okay. So… I have the day off tomorrow. Would you like to meet for breakfast? You know… to talk about the investigation?"

"Sure," she replied and then told him where she was staying.

"Excellent. Right up the road is this little place that has the best breakfast food in town," he said. "It's called the Copper Kettle."

"Yeah, I've seen it." It looked like a small hole-in-the-wall but she enjoyed places like that. Hidden gems with mouthwatering food that usually only the locals knew about.

"How about I pick you up at around nine?"

"Sure," she said and then told him her cabin number.

"Sounds good." He reached into his glove compartment and pulled out a business card. "Call me if something comes up or you have another vision."

"I will," she replied. "I suppose I should give you my number."

"Yeah, that might be a good idea. Here," he handed her his cell phone. "Add yourself to my contact list."

She did what he asked and handed him back his phone.

"Okay, then," he said, putting it away. "Drive safely."

"I will. Thanks, Alex."

"No, thank you. The information you provided is going to help the case. I can feel it in my bones."

Carissa smiled grimly. If only she could do more, like locate the killer before he struck again. Even though she had a feeling he'd eventually end up at Gooseberry Falls, it wasn't as if she could set up camp there and wait for him. "I hope so. Well, goodnight."

"Goodnight."

She got out, closed the door, and got into her SUV. Alex waited for her to start up her vehicle and then they went their separate ways.

She took her time driving back toward the lodge. On the way, Carissa decided to pull into the parking lot of the Gooseberry Falls State Park. She parked, turned off the radio, and then sat there, staring at the pathway leading to the Visitor's Center and falls. For an instant, she thought about getting out and taking it, but knew it would be a waste of time. Nobody was around, it was quieter than a cemetery.

Closing her eyes, she decided to try and meditate, to see if anything new would come to her. Taking deep belly breaths, she inhaled and then exhaled several times, until she felt calm and steady. Carissa then pictured a door opening in her mind, allowing any intuitive messages from beyond to be received. After several seconds, she began to see a butterfly nightlight. Concentrating on the image, Carissa sensed a child sleeping nearby.

Suddenly, Carissa's phone began to ring. Startled, she grabbed it out of her purse and noticed that it was Alex calling.

"Did you make it back to the lodge yet?" he asked.

The tone of his voice gave her goosebumps. "No. Why?"

"A little girl was just reported missing there."

Her heart sank.

Chapter 21

"I DON'T UNDERSTAND. Why did you bring her back to the lodge in the first place? And what happened to Maddy?" asked Rachel as they rushed back to the cabin, trying to find Chloe. Everyone was frantically searching the resort for the missing girl and the police had been called.

"I forgot my keycard on the table, and she came back with me to get yours," he said, looking distraught. "I told her to wait in the lounge—"

"Why would you leave her alone in the lounge?" she cried in disbelief.

"I thought she was safe," he said angrily. "I didn't expect her to run off again."

Rachel frowned. "What do you mean '*again*'?"

"She got mad about something and took off running. That's when I forgot my keycard, trying to chase her down. Hell, maybe she's just hiding out somewhere."

"Could she be with Maddy?"

"Maddy said she hasn't seen her," he said as they climbed the steps to their cabin. "I sent her a text a few minutes ago."

Rachel unlocked the door. "Honey?" She flipped the lights on. "Are you in here?"

"How in the hell would she get inside?" Paul snapped, following her in.

"I don't know. Maybe one of the employees brought her back? And don't you dare snap at me," Rachel said angrily as she moved toward Chloe's bedroom. "You're the one who lost our daughter and you'd better damn well hope we find her."

Swearing, Paul looked around the cabin, hoping that maybe she *was* hiding somewhere.

"She's not here, Paul," cried Rachel, heading back toward the front door. "I'm going to go look down by the lake."

His heart stopped as he imagined Chloe running back there and falling into the cold water. The water was freezing and the waves were so strong, anyone could get pulled under. He followed her back outside and ran into Maddy.

"Have you seen her?" Paul asked tightly.

Maddy had tears in her eyes. "No, Paul. I'm so sorry, I've looked everywhere."

"Dammit, she must still be angry with me. Where in the hell could she have gone?" he said, running a hand through his hair.

"Paul, she's not back here," said Rachel, rushing around the cabin toward them. Seeing Maddy, her face filled with hope. "Did you find her?"

"No," she said. "Not since she was heading back with Paul to the lodge."

"I don't understand any of this. I thought she was going to stay with you, in your cabin?" asked Rachel, on the verge of hysteria.

"Something happened and Chloe became upset," said Maddy.

122

"Nothing *happened*," said Paul icily, glaring at Maddy. "She was just overly tired and had a tantrum."

"Rachel!" cried Mackenzie, racing down the path toward them with Brock close behind. "Did you find her yet?"

"No," said Rachel. She began to cry. "And this isn't like her. She wouldn't hide like this. What if… what if someone took her?"

"Took her? But… I was only gone for a second," Paul said in horror, staring ahead into the darkness.

"That's all anyone would need," said Rachel, now fearing the worst. "They probably walked into the lodge, saw her there, and grabbed her. Oh, my God, someone has my little girl!" she sobbed.

Mackenzie put her arms around Rachel. "Don't worry, Rachel, we'll find her."

"I hope so, Mackenzie, because I couldn't live without her," she squeaked, shaking with fear.

More of the wedding party showed up at the cabin with flashlights, to help search for Chloe.

"We'll split up and look for her in the woods and by the lake," said one of the groomsmen, Tom, who was also Brock's brother.

"Thank you," said Rachel, wiping her tears. "All of you."

"Yes, thank you," said Paul, who was also visibly shaken now.

"Did anyone call the police?" asked Carol, who'd just arrived.

"Yes," said Rachel. "They've been called."

"We also spoke to the manager. In fact, he's heading this way right now," said Brock, waving his thumb.

Rachel turned around and saw a short, squat man rushing toward them wearing a jacket with the lodge's logo.

"Did you find your daughter yet, Mr. and Mrs. Bloom?" he asked.

"No," said Paul.

"I have my staff searching the grounds, too," he said, slightly out of breath. "And the police should be arriving any minute." He looked around the parking lot and toward the woods. "Do you think she could be hiding somewhere?"

"That's what we thought at first," said Rachel. "But, we can't find her anywhere. And, she wouldn't hide outside. She'd be too afraid of the dark."

"I see," he said. "Well then, I'll make sure we do everything we can to try and get her back for you."

"Have you spoken to the front desk attendant?" asked Rachel. "Maybe she saw something?"

"Apparently, Eva had stepped away to use the bathroom when your daughter disappeared," he replied, looking away.

"What about cameras?" asked Paul. "Do you have any in the lounge? If someone took her, we can see who it was."

"Yes, as a matter of fact we do, and I was just going to suggest that," said the manager.

"Wait a second," said Rachel, thinking back to earlier. "What about the swimming pool? She desperately wanted to go swimming earlier. Maybe she took off and is playing around by the pool?"

"I can't believe I didn't think about checking there," said Paul. "I'll go and check."

"We close and lock the pool area at eleven," said the manager as Paul raced away. "I doubt he'll find her there, but I guess it's still worth checking out."

"We can't afford to leave any rock unturned," said Carol, turning to Rachel. "Don't worry, with all of us working together, we'll find your daughter. I mean, she couldn't be too far, right? The roads are bad, so if anyone did take her, they must be close by."

Rachel, who was crying again, just nodded.

"Mrs. Bloom, if you'd like to come with me, we can check the video footage from my office," said the manager. "Hopefully, it picked up what happened."

"Okay," said Rachel.

"Wait a second. What about the photographer?" asked Maddy, who'd been silent for most of the time. "Harold? He was out here when Chloe ran away from us. I hate to even suggest this but... maybe he took her?"

"No, I can't imagine Harold doing something like that," said the resort manager. "He's an upstanding citizen. A school teacher. He's not a kidnapper."

"Maybe, but if he was one of the last people to see my daughter, and we don't find her soon, I want him questioned," said Rachel. "Along with everyone else at this resort. Someone has *got* to know where she is or who might have taken her."

Chapter 22

CARISSA ARRIVED BACK at the resort the same time two squad cars pulled into the parking lot. Although it was after midnight, the place was alive with people carrying flashlights and searching everywhere for the missing child.

She parked her vehicle and quickly went to find the girl's parents. Rushing into the lodge, she asked the front desk attendant where they might be.

"The mother is in with the manager, looking through video coverage. I'm not sure where her husband is. Are you with the wedding party?"

"No," she replied. "I'm a friend. Where's the manager's office?"

"Down that hallway and to the left," said the young woman.

Carissa turned and began walking that way when she heard the police officers step into the lodge. She wanted to talk to the parents before they monopolized the rest of their time.

Finding the manager's office, she knocked on the door loudly.

"Yes?" called a man's voice.

Carissa opened up the door and stuck her head inside. "Excuse me, I'm looking for the missing girl's mother. I heard she might be in here?"

"That's me," said an attractive woman who looked close to Carissa's age. There was mascara running down her face and it was obvious the woman was distraught.

"Hi," she said, stepping inside. She closed the door behind her. "My name is Carissa Jones and... I think that I can help you find your daughter."

Chapter 23

RACHEL STARED AT the woman, a feeling of hope bubbling inside of her.

"Have you seen her?" she asked, standing up.

"Yes and no," said the stranger, with an apologetic smile. "Not in the way you're thinking."

Rachel frowned. "What do you know about my daughter?"

The woman licked her lips. "A man kidnapped her and I think we can find her if you'll let me help."

"A man? *Who*?" asked Rachel, her eyes flashing angrily.

Before Carissa could answer, there was another knock on the door.

"Mr. Johnson, the police are here to talk to Mrs. Bloom," said a woman from the other side of the door.

"She'll be right there, Eva," he replied, staring at Carissa curiously.

"Okay, I'll let them know," she replied.

"Who has my daughter?" asked Rachel, shaking. "Please, tell me."

"I… don't know exactly. He thinks your daughter is his, though, Mrs. Bloom. And that's both good and bad. He won't harm her until he realizes she's not the one he wants."

Rachel was beginning to wonder if the woman was crazy. "I don't understand. How do you know all of this?"

"I'm a psychic."

Sighing, Rachel sank back down into the chair. "Oh, God," she said, closing her eyes. "And I thought you could actually help us locate Chloe."

"I can. Listen to me," said Carissa, walking over to her. She kneeled down. "I have helped locate missing children before. In fact, I drove all the way from the cities to help you find her before he hurts her."

That got Rachel's attention. "Hurt her? He's going to hurt my baby?"

Carissa nodded. She didn't want to sugarcoat anything. She needed to light a fire under this woman's feet so they could work together before her daughter was killed. "Believe me, he will kill her if we don't act now."

Rachel's hands began to tremble. "Wait a second. She just disappeared. How did you know she was going to go missing?"

"I'm a pre-cog. I sometimes dream about things before they happen. Tell me something – your daughter has long blonde hair, blue eyes, and round cheeks. She loves to collect rocks and wanted to go swimming earlier…"

"Yes. How did you know that?" Her eyes narrowed. "Were you spying on us?"

"No. Like I said before, I'm a psychic and this stuff just comes to me." She grabbed Rachel's hand and closed her eyes. "You and your husband haven't been getting along. He... he's been..." Carissa suddenly opened her eyes. Her husband was cheating on her. "I'm... sorry, Rachel."

"He's been *what*?" she snapped. "What are you trying to say?"

There was no way Carissa was going to go down that road with her. The woman's husband needed to be the one to tell her. "He's keeping something from you. I won't tell you what that is, because it's not my business, but it has to do with why your daughter disappeared tonight."

Rachel's face was so pale, she looked like a ghost. "I don't want to believe you, but... it's hard not to. Paul told me that she was angry with him, but he wouldn't tell me why exactly."

"This is ridiculous," said the manager, coming to life. "She's obviously a fraud. Don't listen to her, Mrs. Bloom. If she knows where your daughter is, it's because she's involved somehow. Hell, maybe this is about getting a ransom and she's here to feel you out?"

Carissa glared at him. "Wow. You're really something. I'm *not* involved and you should be ashamed of yourself, Mr. Johnson. If you wouldn't have been fooling around with your attendant when she should have been minding the front desk, the child might not be missing right in the first place."

The manager stared at her in stunned silence.

"Is that true?" asked Rachel, looking at him.

The guilty expression on his face was all the answer she needed.

"Yeah, I thought so," said Carissa and then turned to look at Rachel again. "Now, let me help you locate your little girl."

"Okay," she replied. "I'm willing to do everything it takes to find her. Where do we start?"

Before Carissa could explain, there was a loud rap on the door.

"Police. Open up," said a firm voice.

Chapter 24

PAUL FELT LIKE he was on the verge of a nervous breakdown when he couldn't find Chloe in the pool area. Deeply ashamed of himself and his stupidity, he headed to the front desk, hoping there was some better news to be found.

"Where's the manager?" he asked the attendant, a woman named Eva.

"In his office with your wife, Mr. Bloom. It's down the hallway," she told him. "The police just arrived, too."

"Thanks," he said, turning around.

When he arrived at the manager's office, the door was open and two officers were inside questioning his wife. There was also another woman, whom he didn't recognize.

"My husband was the last one to see her," Rachel said, noticing his approach.

The officers turned to him. They introduced themselves and then began asking questions about Chloe.

"So, you left her in the lounge," said the taller of the two cops, Officer Reynolds. "Was there anyone else around?"

"No," he replied. "Looking back, I realize it was a horrible mistake, but I was only gone for a couple of minutes. My wife couldn't find her keycard in her purse right away and so it took me—"

"Don't you dare put this on me!" snapped Rachel. Paul was always giving her crap about being disorganized. "You shouldn't have left her alone in the first place."

"I know," he said angrily. "I'm not blaming you for it. I'm just trying to give them an idea of how long I was gone."

"How long do you think you were away from your daughter?" asked the shorter cop, Officer Smith.

"Four minutes, tops," he replied.

"A lot can happen in one minute, let alone four," said Officer Reynolds. "Are you sure you don't remember seeing someone leave the bar or pass anyone in the hallway on your way to find your wife?"

Paul squeezed the bridge of his nose as he tried thinking back. "To be honest, I didn't notice anyone coming or going. I was in a hurry and just wanted to get back to Chloe."

"What about the front desk clerk?" asked Officer Reynolds, looking around. "Did she see anything?"

"Apparently, she was busy," said Rachel dryly.

The manager cleared his throat. "We were having a meeting," said the man, his face turning a bright red.

"And there was nobody else tending the counter?" asked Officer Smith.

"No," said the manager. "It's pretty slow here at night and we usually only have one attendant working the counter."

"Are there cameras in the lounge?" asked Officer Smith.

"Yes. In fact, we were just about to go over them," replied the manager, motioning toward his laptop.

"Okay. Let's have a look at your footage," said Officer Reynolds.

As they were preparing the clip, Paul noticed Carissa standing there, watching silently.

"I'm sorry, who are you?" he asked, wondering if she worked for the hotel or was with the police.

"My name is Carissa Jones," she said. "I'm here to help you find your daughter."

"She's a psychic," said the manager dryly.

Paul stared at her in disbelief, and then snorted.

"No need to be rude," said Rachel. "Anyone willing to help us find Chloe should be thanked and not scorned."

Paul looked at Carissa. "Sorry, I've had a rough night."

"I understand," she replied.

"By the way, you never did give me a good explanation as to why Chloe was so angry with you in the first place," said Rachel, watching him closely.

"I don't remember. It was something stupid," Paul said, avoiding her eyes.

"Okay," said the manager. "Here we go."

Everyone stared at the computer screen. On the footage, Chloe had her back to the camera and was sitting on the sofa. A few seconds after, a man approached her. He wore some kind of dark parka and a hoodie underneath, which covered his hair.

Rachel gasped. "Oh, my God."

"Son of a bitch," growled Paul, watching as the man offered Chloe his hand.

"Freeze the frame," said Reynolds quickly.

The manager paused it.

Reynolds moved closer to the screen. "Okay, play it very slowly now."

The manager did what he was told and the footage resumed in slow motion.

"It looks like he's definitely avoiding the camera," said Reynolds, glancing at the other cop.

"Yes," agreed Smith.

The man offered his hand to Chloe again and said something else. Whatever it was, it changed her mind. She took it, stood up, and left with him. Unfortunately, his back was to the camera the entire time.

"All that and we don't know what the bastard looked like," muttered Paul. "Is that the only camera you have in the lounge? Don't you have anything facing the opposite direction?"

"No," said the manager.

"I can't believe that monster has my little girl," said Rachel, now weeping openly.

Carissa handed her several tissues from the manager's desk.

"Thank you," said Rachel, taking them.

"What about outside? Are there cameras in the parking lot?" asked Paul angrily.

"Yes," replied the manager. "Just one in each lot, though. Hopefully we'll pick something up."

"Play that again for us first," said Smith.

The manager rewound the video.

"Is there anything that looks familiar about him?" asked Reynolds.

135

"There's not much to see," muttered Paul.

"I'm talking about his jacket or what he was wearing," replied Reynolds, glancing back at him.

"I doubt that I've ever seen him before," said Paul. "But who's to say?"

"I don't recognize him," said the manager.

Everyone looked at Rachel.

"No. He could be anybody," she said, sounding defeated.

"Well, it's definitely not Harold," said Paul. "I guess we can rule him out."

"Yes. Harold is obviously heavier and that guy seems like he'd be younger," said Rachel.

"I wonder if he's a guest here?" said Smith. "You mentioned that you were here for a wedding?"

"Yes," said Rachel. "My best friend's, Mackenzie."

Smith scratched his chin. "It's possible that he's here for the same thing, and that's how he may have spotted your daughter."

"We definitely need to search the cabins," said the other cop. "I should get on that now."

"And issue an Amber Alert," said Smith, looking over his shoulder.

"I'm on it," Reynolds replied and left the office.

"The fact that this guy was avoiding the camera shows he knew about it," said Smith, pointing to the screen. "Maybe he's an employee?"

"It's not exactly a hidden camera," said the manager with a frown. "Anyone could spot it. Especially someone who is up to no good."

Rachel stood up and began to pace. "I feel like we're running out of time." She looked over at Carissa. "After seeing that clip, do you think you know who he is?"

Carissa shook her head. "No, but I believe it's related to the little girl they found earlier today."

Rachel frowned. "What little girl?"

Carissa told her about the child who'd been found in Lutsen earlier. "I think it's the same guy."

Horrified, Rachel sank to her knees. "Oh, my God, Paul!" she sobbed.

Chapter 25

CARISSA HADN'T WANTED to be the one to tell them, but in her heart she knew that the crimes were related.

Paul reached for his wife and took her into his arms. "Why didn't you tell us about this?" he asked the cops angrily.

"We weren't sure if that case had anything to do with your missing daughter," said Smith. "And we certainly didn't want to panic anyone."

"It's the same guy," said Carissa bluntly.

Everyone looked at her.

"Excuse me, but can I see some identification?" asked the cop.

Before she could respond, Alex and Jim appeared in the doorway.

Carissa relaxed.

"Hey, Jim," said Smith.

As the sheriff introduced himself to Paul and Rachel, Alex edged his way over to Carissa.

"I take it their daughter is still missing?" he asked.

Carissa nodded.

"Is it the girl from your dreams?" he asked quietly.

"Yes. Her mother showed me a picture. It's definitely her," she replied grimly.

She hadn't ever met Chloe but now that she knew the girl was real, Carissa couldn't help but feel partially responsible for her abduction. Especially now, knowing that the girl had been staying at the same resort.

"I was just asking her for some I.D.," said Smith, motioning toward Carissa.

"I already did that a couple of hours ago," said Jim. "She's just someone trying to help. So," he turned to the manager, "you have video footage?"

They watched the video again and the sheriff took his turn questioning the couple.

"Do you think it's the same man who killed the other little girl in Lutsen?" asked Rachel, wiping fresh tears with a tissue.

"We don't know for sure, but… my gut says that it probably is," said Jim somberly. "It's too coincidental."

Rachel looked at Carissa. "You have to help us find our daughter."

"I'll do whatever I can," she replied.

Jim looked at Carissa. "By the way, we think we have a positive I.D. on the other girl. Her parents are going to verify it, but you were right about what you said. The child's name was Amy and she was from Duluth. She'd been missing since last weekend."

Carissa nodded. "What about the friend? Was there another girl he released?"

Jim nodded. "Yes. Hopefully we can get ahold of her and find out if she remembers anything more about the assailant."

Rachel perked up. "Are you saying that you might have a suspect soon?"

"I hope so. I can only promise that we'll do our best to catch this guy and bring your daughter back. Fortunately, Ms. Jones has given us several… unexplainable tips," he replied. "I never thought I'd be saying this, but, you definitely have my attention."

"Thank you. I'm going to try and meditate, to see if anything new comes to me," she replied.

"Let me know if you do," said Jim.

Carissa nodded.

"Oh, for God's sake, you don't believe this woman is really a psychic, do you?" muttered Paul.

"Actually, yes, I do. Like you, I doubted her at first, too. But, she definitely knows things, Mr. Bloom," said Jim. "Things she shouldn't. Whatever kind of sixth sense she has, it should be taken seriously."

Rolling his eyes, he shook his head.

"I believe in you," said Rachel, looking at Carissa.

"Thank you," she replied.

"So do I," said Alex.

Carissa smiled.

"That other little girl. The one that they found earlier," said Rachel, looking at Jim. "Was she… molested?"

"She was found naked but we don't know for sure if the kidnapper sexually assaulted her," he replied.

Rachel's lips began to tremble. She covered her face. "Oh, God."

"If he touches Chloe, I'll kill the bastard with my own two hands," said Paul, so angry that he was shaking again.

Carissa sighed. "He didn't touch her in that way. He's not interested in that."

"So, why is he doing this?" asked Paul, looking at her. "If you know so much about this asshole, tell us why."

"He's looking for his daughter," said Carissa, understanding his anger but not appreciating his rudeness. She really didn't like Paul. "And, right now, he thinks Chloe is her."

"The sick bastard," muttered Paul.

"The good news is that while he believes this, he'll be good to her," said Carissa. "But, eventually, he'll figure out that she's not who he wants her to be and that's why we have to move fast."

"What will he do to her," squeaked Rachel, "when he realizes she's not his daughter?"

"Nothing good," Carissa replied.

Chapter 26

WHEN THEY CHECKED the video footage of the parking lot again, the kidnapper had kept his face down.

"Did you see that? They stopped for a minute and I think she might have pointed at our cabin," said Paul, leaning toward the screen.

"That's where she thought he was taking her," said Carissa, the knowledge hitting her quickly.

"So, then why did she go with him into the parking lot?" mumbled Paul.

"That's a good question. Any ideas?" asked Jim, looking at Carissa.

"I don't know. He must have lied to her," she replied.

"I just don't understand why she left with him so easily," said Rachel. "I taught her better than that."

"Maybe she knows him?" said Jim. "Do you recognize *anything* about the man? Like the way he walks or if there any other physical characteristics that look familiar?" asked Jim.

"The only thing I can tell is that he's slim and maybe my height," said Paul. "Other than that, there is not a whole lot to look at."

Alex glanced at Carissa.

She shrugged. There wasn't anything distinguishable about the kidnapper for her either.

Unfortunately, the guy had also parked beyond the camera range, so they weren't able to get a look at his vehicle.

"Look. There's Paul," said Rachel, pointing toward the screen. They watched as he stepped outside.

"Jesus, I *just* missed them?" he said angrily. "Are you kidding me?"

"Did you see anyone get into a vehicle?" asked Jim.

He rubbed his forehead. "I… I'm trying to remember. I called her name and nobody answered. Wait a second." His eyes widened. "I did see someone in the parking lot. He was standing in the back, next to a car but I only glanced at him for a second. I was too busy looking for Chloe. I thought she'd run off, to be honest. The idea of someone kidnapping her never even crossed my mind at that point."

"Could you tell what kind of car it was?" asked the sheriff.

"No. It was too dark and I only glanced his way for a second. I can't believe I was that close to them," he said in a hoarse voice.

"She didn't yell out your name?" asked Jim.

"Not that I heard," he replied, his eyes filling with tears.

"She couldn't," said Carissa, her eyes looking somewhere far away. "He put a rag over her mouth. She passed out."

"The bastard," said Paul, who'd finally reached his breaking point. He buried his face into his hands and began to sob.

Chapter 27

AN AMBER ALERT was issued for Chloe and the police began interviewing both guests and employees. A new, larger search party was formed, and although it was late, some of the townspeople heard about the missing child and volunteered to look for her as well.

"One of you should go back to the cabin," said Jim, talking to Chloe's parents. "And keep your phones nearby. Does your daughter know how to use a telephone?"

"Yes," said Rachel.

"Good. If, by the grace of God, she gets away from him, she might try calling you," said Jim.

Rachel nodded.

"You mentioned something earlier about Gooseberry Falls. I sent one of my deputies over to check it out," Jim said to Carissa. "In an unmarked squad car. He's going to keep an eye on things for a while and call me if something comes up."

"Good," she replied.

Jim looked at the manager. "I want a list of every employee who was working today. I'll need their address, phone numbers, and the hours they put in."

144

"I highly doubt one of my people did this," said Mr. Johnson.

"Let's hope not but we can't rule anyone out," he replied.

"Maybe you should have Carissa sit in while some of the people are being interviewed," suggested Alex. "I know that's unorthodox, but she might pick up on something."

He nodded. "I suppose it's possible that someone saw something and she might be able to probe their brains. It could take all night, though."

"I don't know if I can probe anyone's brains, but if you don't mind, I would definitely like sit in," Carissa said with a little smile.

"Sure," he replied.

Reynolds stepped back into the office. "The FBI is here," he said.

"I was wondering when they were going to show," muttered Jim. He sighed. "I should go and talk to them. Obviously, they'll be wanting to interview you as well."

"Sure," said Paul, running a hand through his hair. "Maybe we'll have a better chance of finding our daughter with them onboard."

"I don't know about better, but when it comes to a missing child, joining forces certainly can't hurt," Jim replied.

Carissa was relieved to see that the sheriff wasn't against the FBI getting involved. She knew that sometimes local authorities took offense when the bureau jumped in to help. She only hoped that the agents would allow her to stay onboard.

"Alex," said Jim, as they made their way to the lounge, "You know you don't have to stay. I know it's been a long day for you and I can keep you updated, if you want to go and get some sleep."

"No way. I couldn't sleep even if I tried, to be honest," he replied.

"You and me both," said Jim.

When the group arrived back at the front desk, two agents were waiting for them. Jim introduced himself and then everyone else.

"I'm Special Agent Carrie Frost," said a woman, who looked to be in her late twenties. Her brown hair was pulled tightly into a bun, making her eyes look almost cat-like. "And this is Special Agent Rick Mars. I know you've probably gone over what happened several times tonight, Mr. and Mrs. Bloom, but we need to hear the story directly from you."

"No problem," said Paul. "And can I just say that I'm relieved you're here. Not that I don't trust the local police, but I just feel more comfortable knowing the FBI is here to handle this."

"We certainly appreciate your confidence in us and will do everything we can to get your daughter back." Agent Frost looked at the manager. "Is there a place we can begin interviewing people?"

"Yes," he said. "You can use the conference room." He pointed. "It's down that hallway. The door is unlocked."

"Thank you," she replied.

While Rachel and Paul followed the agents, Carissa walked over to the sofa where Chloe had been sitting. She sat down and looked up at the enormous mounted grizzly bear by the fireplace. Closing her eyes, she tried to envision what Chloe had been thinking and feeling when the kidnapper had approached her.

"Are you getting anything?" asked Alex, standing behind her.

She opened her eyes and looked over her shoulder at him. "Not yet."

"Sorry," he replied, smiling sheepishly. "I'll leave you alone. Carry on."

Carissa tried again. After a few minutes of concentration, she began to pick up some things. First was that Chloe had still been angry with her father when she was waiting in the lounge. Secondly, she'd believed that her father had sent the man to take her back to the cabin. Opening her eyes, she told Alex.

"That explains why she walked out with him so easily," he replied.

"There's something else I'm picking up on," she murmured, remembering what the parents had said. Chloe had thrown some kind of temper tantrum. "I think I know why Chloe threw a fit earlier."

Alex walked around and sat down on the sofa. "Why?"

"She saw something that disturbed her," Carissa whispered. "Something with her dad. I actually felt it when I was standing next to him."

"Rachel did mention that Chloe was supposed to stay overnight with Maddy and then it didn't happen." Alex's eyes widened. "You don't think…"

Carissa nodded. "Yes. I actually do think she may have seen Paul doing something inappropriate with Maddy. That's why she took off on him. Paul knows, too, and doesn't want Rachel to find out."

"Wow, you picked up all of that?"

She nodded.

"I guess it doesn't surprise me. He's kind of a dick," said Alex.

She agreed.

The front door opened and an older man rushed inside. He walked over to where Jim was talking to Mr. Johnson and asked where Paul and Rachel Bloom were.

"They're in the conference room talking to the FBI," said Jim, who was drinking a cup of coffee. "I'm Sheriff Jim Collins. Who might you be?"

"My name is Harold Williams. I heard about their little girl," he said, looking distraught. "I think I might have some information that could help."

"What kind of information?" he asked.

"I was in the parking lot, brushing the snow off of my car, when I noticed a man walking into the lounge. This was shortly after I'd run into Chloe and her father. The poor thing had fallen onto the ice. Anyway, I didn't think much of it until Mackenzie called and told me what happened. Thinking back, this guy looked a little suspicious."

Alex and Carissa got up from the sofa and walked over to them.

"I take it you didn't see this guy leave with Chloe?" asked the sheriff.

"No, I left about a minute after he walked into the lodge," he replied.

"What was he wearing?" asked Jim.

"A black winter jacket. He had a grey hoodie on underneath that was pulled over his head," said Harold. "I didn't get a good look at his face, but I knew which car was his. I'd seen him digging around in the trunk earlier."

"Harold, I could kiss you right now," said the Sheriff, taking out his notepad. "What kind was it?"

"Chevy Impala. A newer model," he replied. "It was red."

Alex frowned.

"You sure about that?" said Mr. Johnson, looking shocked. "A red Impala?"

"Yes," replied Harold.

"You know who he is," said Carissa.

The manager nodded.

Chapter 28

CHLOE WOKE UP. Her head was throbbing and she felt dizzy. Wincing, she cried out for her mother.

In answer, a dog began to bark somewhere.

Startled, Chloe's eyes adjusted to the darkness. She looked around and realized that she wasn't in the cabin but some strange bedroom. She wondered if she was in Maddy's cabin, but then the memories came rushing back and she began to tremble.

The man from the lodge had lied to her.

She remembered walking outside with him, toward the parking lot, and then her father calling her name. After that, she wasn't sure what happened, only that she was somewhere scary and wanted to go home.

Terrified, Chloe got out of the bed and tiptoed over to the door. Turning on the light, she looked around the bedroom and was shocked. It was actually a very nice room and reminded her a little of the one she had at home, only this one had white furniture and a pink comforter. There were dolls and stuffed animals on a nearby shelf, an easel, a caddy with paint supplies, and a toy box at the end of the bed with the name "Faith" engraved on the top.

Turning around, she tried opening up the door, but found that it was locked.

"Mommy!" she called, hoping that maybe she'd been wrong and her mother was in the house somewhere.

She heard a noise from above and then footsteps. Backing away, Chloe stared at the door, frightened of who might be coming for her.

"Mommy?" she whispered, her lips quivering.

She heard an upstairs door opening and then heavy footsteps climbing down a creaky staircase. A dog was with the person, barking frantically. Chloe was so terrified, she got back into the bed and pulled the covers over her head.

"Maisie, settle down," said a familiar voice.

Recognizing the voice, Chloe's heart sank. She peeked out from under the blanket as the man from the resort unlocked the door. A small dog raced into the bedroom, running straight for her. It jumped onto the bed and began climbing all over her, making Chloe giggle. It began licking her hand and she threw her arms around the dog, hugging it.

"That's Maisie," he said, standing in the doorway.

"Where's my mommy and daddy?" she asked, trembling.

He sighed and walked into the bedroom. "I see they've really brainwashed you well."

"Huh?" she asked, not understanding.

He sat down on the bed next to her. "Your name is not Chloe. It's Faith."

Staring at him, she shook her head. "No."

He grabbed her hand and stared into her eyes. "Yes. You're my daughter and… this is your dog, now. Maisie." He grinned. "I bought her for you."

She began to cry. What he was saying didn't make any sense. "I want my mommy."

His smile fell. "Your mommy took you from me. You don't want her. She's a horrible woman."

Chloe began crying harder.

He sighed. "Look," he said, wiping her wet cheek with his thumb. "I know this is a lot for you to handle right now, but you have to realize that those people you were with are not your parents. I'm your father and now we can finally be together. You and me."

"I want my daddy," she cried, getting out of the bed.

Clenching his jaw, he grabbed her arms and shook her. "I'm right here," he snapped. "I'm your daddy. Me!"

Maisie jumped off the bed and began barking at the man.

"Shut up," he said and then kicked the Beagle.

The dog yelped and ran off.

Terrified beyond belief, Chloe closed her eyes and sobbed. She was going to die, she just knew it.

"Faith! Look at me," growled the man. He shook her again. "Open up your eyes!"

She did and the look on his face made her pee her pants.

"I don't want to hurt you," he said, his eyes boring into hers. "Do you believe me?"

She nodded in fear.

He relaxed. "You made me kick Maisie. That was *your* fault."

Chloe looked at the puppy. Her tail was tucked and she was trembling by the doorway.

"Now, I know it's going to take some time for me to fix what those people did to you, but you need to know that sometimes I get very angry but... I don't want to hurt you." His eyes softened. "I love you, Faith."

She just stared at him.

"Tell me that you love me, too," he said, his grip tightening.

"I love you, too," she squeaked.

"I love you, *Daddy*," he said firmly.

Chloe could barely see him through her tears. "I love you, Daddy," she repeated.

He grinned and stood up. "Good. Now, are you hungry? I know it's late, but a little ice cream never hurt anyone, right?"

She was too afraid to say anything and just nodded.

"Good. You're going to have to stay down here. You can eat over there for now," he said, pointing to the small pink table and chair set.

Chloe nodded.

"I'll be right back," he replied. "In the meantime, I know that you had an accident and I'm not mad, okay?"

She just stared at him.

He sighed and pointed at the dresser. "There are some pajamas in the top drawer. Why don't you go into the bathroom, clean yourself up, and put those on?"

"Okay," she said in a hoarse voice, afraid to disobey him.

His face softened. "Look, we may have started out on the wrong foot, but I promise you, honey, we're going to be very happy together. Especially in Alaska."

153

Her breath caught in her throat. "Alaska?"

He grinned. "Yes, isn't that exciting? Fresh air, wildlife, and," his smile widened, "I'm going to find work as a prospector. Do you know what that is?"

She shook her head.

His eyes widened. "Haven't you ever seen those shows on television? About gold mining? The ones on the Discovery Channel?"

Chloe remembered her father watching something like that but was too afraid to tell the man. "No."

"That's okay. Just know that I'm going to take good care of you, Faith. In fact, we'll be leaving tomorrow before noon. Don't worry," he nodded toward her pants, "we'll get you some new clothes on the way up there. I've been planning this for a very long time."

Chloe felt like the floor had dropped from under her. He was taking her someplace far, where her parents would never, ever be able to find her.

"I'll be back. Come on, Maisie," he said. "I'll give you a treat, too. You deserve one."

The man left the bedroom with Maisie at his heels. He locked the door and went back upstairs.

Trembling, Chloe went over to the dresser and pulled out a pair of princess pajamas. She took them into the bathroom, locked the door, and did what he'd ordered her to do.

Chapter 29

AFTER LEAVING FAITH alone in the bedroom, he hurried upstairs to get her some ice cream. Although, admittedly he'd lost his temper, he felt that they'd made a connection at the very end.

"Here, Maisie," he said, reaching into the dog treat canister. He threw her a big Milk-Bone and then brushed the crumbs off of his hand using his jeans.

Maisie grabbed the treat and took it to her dog bed.

"Sorry about earlier," he said, grabbing a bowl out of the cupboard. "Things got a little intense. I suppose I should probably take my pills. I can't let my temper get the best of me."

The dog didn't look up from her treat.

Sighing, he went over to the freezer to grab the container of chocolate-chip ice cream, when his cell phone began to ring.

"Shit," he mumbled, pulling it out of his hoodie. He knew it was late, so the call was probably from work. They were already going to start questioning him. Surprisingly, enough, it wasn't the lodge. It was his cousin.

"Hey, what's up?" he asked, shocked to be getting a call from the guy. They hadn't spoken in ages.

"What in the hell have you done?"

His heart skipped a beat. "I don't know what you mean."

"I've been trying to call you all night, dammit, why didn't you answer?"

"I was working."

"Let me guess, Superior Views Resort?"

He broke out into a cold sweat. He knew his plans were already screwed. Of course his cousin would have figured everything out. "Yes. I bartend there on the weekends. I told you that a while ago."

"Jesus, I didn't want to believe that you were capable of this," he said angrily. "I tried telling myself that there was no way you could be involved. No way! Obviously, I was wrong."

He looked out the window, afraid that he'd see headlights already pulling into the driveway. "I don't know what you're talking about. Involved with what?"

"Cut the bullshit. Where is the girl?"

"Who?"

"Chloe, dammit! What have you done with her?"

"Chloe? Who's that?" he asked, still pulling at strings even though he knew it was pointless.

"No more lies. Jesus, Ben, how could you do this? They were just innocent little girls."

Ben closed his eyes, trying to block out the images of the girls he'd had to kill. "I didn't do anything."

"I'm coming over. Don't you dare leave your house," he growled and then hung up.

"Shit," he muttered. Ben shoved his phone back into his hoodie and raced downstairs. He unlocked the door and noticed that Faith was still in the bathroom. He rushed over and pounded on the door. "Faith, are you finished in there?"

The door opened slowly and she stared up at him with frightened eyes.

"Sorry about this but we have a change of plans," he said. "We're leaving right now."

Chapter 30

JIM TOLD THE FBI what he'd learned and they put an All-Points Bulletin out for Ben Frazer, one of the part-time bartenders.

"The address we have is registered under his mother's name," said Jim, scratching his chin.

"She passed away a couple of years ago," said the manager, still shocked. "At least, that's what he told me."

"I'm heading over there," said Jim, digging into his pocket for his keys.

Paul zipped up his jacket. "I'm coming with you."

"No. You stay here," Jim replied, heading toward the doorway with the Feds. He looked over his shoulder. "Don't worry. Once we get your little girl back, I'll call you."

"This is bullshit," said Paul, watching as the police and FBI stepped out of the lodge. "Chloe is going to be frightened. What if something goes wrong? What if she gets hurt?"

"Listen," said Alex. "I don't want to put a damper on things, but it's highly unlikely that Ben Frazer is waiting around at home for the cops to show up. I'd bet money on it that he's on his way out of town."

Paul sat down and rubbed his face. "Thanks for the encouraging words," he said dryly.

Alex took out his truck keys. "I'm going to follow them out there and I'll keep you guys posted myself."

"Thank you," said Rachel.

"Screw the police. I should follow you," said Paul, standing back up. "Waiting here is going to drive me insane and Chloe is going to need one of her parents there."

"Both of her parents," added Rachel.

"No," said Alex. "You might get in the way and the sheriff would be furious if you showed up. And like I said, I doubt he's waiting around to be arrested."

"Fine," Paul mumbled, looking deflated.

Carissa followed Alex to the door. "Call me as soon as you find out anything."

"Will do," he said, pulling his keys out of his jacket pocket. "And let me know if you find out anything new, okay?"

She nodded.

Once Alex left the building, Rachel asked Carissa what she thought of the situation.

"To be honest, I think that Alex might be right," she said, wishing that she felt more positive about what was happening. "I feel like they're wasting time looking there, too. But, who knows? They might find something that could them help locate Ben and Chloe."

"This is maddening," said Rachel, staring off into space. "I feel like we should be doing something more than just sitting around here."

"Me, too," mumbled Paul.

"At least they know who he is," said Carissa.

"Yeah," Rachel replied. She looked at Paul and their eyes met. "I just hope he doesn't do anything to our baby."

Paul's face filled with fear. He walked over and put his arms around Rachel. "He does and I don't care if I go to prison. I'll make sure the piece of shit never touches anyone ever again."

***

Twenty minutes later and there was still no word from Jim or Alex.

"I swear if we don't hear something soon, I'm going to jump in my truck and start searching this town myself."

Carissa was also beginning to feel the same way.

"I'm going back to the cabin to change," he said, putting his jacket on.

"Me, too," said Rachel, who was still dressed up from earlier. She looked at Carissa. "We'll catch up with you soon?"

"Sure," she replied.

The couple left and Carissa sat down on the sofa. Staring into the fire, she felt like she was missing something. Something important.

"Excuse me."

Carissa looked up and saw an attractive young woman in her twenties standing next to her. She recognized her as one of the bartenders.

She smiled grimly. "I'm sorry to bother you. I saw you with the police earlier. I know you're helping with the case."

"Yes."

"My name is Janet. I just heard about Ben," she said. "We work together, you know? I just can't believe he could do something like that."

"People used to surprise me all the time. Not anymore," admitted Carissa. There were a lot of deep, dark secrets out there and there were times when she wished that she didn't have psychic abilities.

"We went out a couple of times. Just as friends, though," said Janet, sitting down next to her. "I just can't believe he could harm a child. Did he really kidnap and murder that other little girl they found in Lutsen?"

"I think so," she replied, although her intuition said that it was indeed Ben.

"Wow," she shuddered. "That's just creepy."

Carissa nodded. "Do you know if Ben was married before or had a daughter?"

"If he did, he never mentioned it to me. He dated a lot though. Rather, I should say he 'hooked up' a lot."

Carissa remembered seeing Ben smiling flirtatiously at her from behind the bar. She could definitely see him being a player.

Janet stared into the fire. "Now, thinking back, I almost feel like he was trying to prove something to himself. Like, he wanted to prove to himself that he could have anyone he wanted. Even married women weren't off limits."

"Really?"

"Yeah. He was always leaving with women at the end of the night it seemed. More than once, I saw a woman leave with her husband and then return later, alone. They'd go out to his vehicle and... well, you know."

"Have sex," said Carissa.

"Yes. He'd never admit to it outright, but we knew what was going on."

Carissa suddenly got the impression that Ben had been trying to fill the void his estranged wife had created. She'd left and taken his daughter away, making him feel empty and alone. The challenge of trying to bed a multitude of women, and scoring, might have eased the pain, if only for a short time.

"Sounds like Ben is a very busy guy," Carissa said dryly.

"Yeah, and not just in that capacity. I'm surprised he has time for women. Although he works here part-time during the day he's a full-time gym teacher at the elementary school up the road. He also coaches soccer," said Janet.

That explained how he'd met Amy, the soccer player. She must have caught his eye at one of the games.

"Is there anything else about Ben that you can remember?" asked Carissa.

"Not really. I mean, I don't know if this helps at all but he's not a drinker or a smoker. In fact, the guy was very health conscious. He belonged to a gym, too."

"Do you think he took steroids?" Carissa asked.

"I don't think so, although… obviously, he has a lot of secrets that none of us knew about."

Carissa nodded.

"Well, I was just heading out. I hope they find the little girl. I feel just awful for her parents," said Janet, standing up.

"I know, me too. Oh, one more thing - did you know if Ben had any other family that he might have mentioned?"

She bit her lower lip and then nodded. "Actually, yeah, a cousin. They weren't on speaking terms."

"Why?"

"I think it had something to do with the man's wife. Maybe she wasn't off limits either," Janet said dryly.

The final piece of the puzzle suddenly snapped into place and Carissa gasped in horror.

"What's wrong?" asked Janet.

"I have to go," she said standing up quickly.

"Did I say something wrong?"

Ignoring her, Carissa ran out of the lodge and headed to her SUV.

Chapter 31

BEN PACKED QUICKLY, made a little makeshift bed for Faith in the van, and then put both her and Maisie inside.

"It's going to be a little bumpy," he said. "Just lie down and try to sleep if you can. We have a long drive ahead of us."

Faith stared at him with such sadness that it made his heart heavy. She had no idea how great he was going to make life for her. She just needed to give him a chance.

"Don't worry, pumpkin. We're going to have a wonderful life together," he said, trying to reassure her. "I promise."

"I want my mommy," she replied in a frightened voice.

Sighing in irritation, he slammed the back door and went around the van. He climbed inside and started the engine, praying that his cousin didn't suddenly show up to confront him. He didn't want to shoot the guy, but there was no way he'd allow anyone to take Faith from him again.

"And… we're off," he said, giving one last look at his in-law's cabin. Barbara's parents were both long gone and they'd left her the place. On the run from Ben, she'd never returned, however, so he'd taken it over. Nobody but his cousin knew about the cabin,

164

and Ben assumed his mother's address would be the first place he'd check. At least he hoped that was the case.

Unfortunately, he was wrong.

"Oh, shit," mumbled Ben, slamming on the brakes. A vehicle had just turned into the private dirt road and was coming in quickly. From the shape of the headlights and how erratically the person was driving, he knew it was his cousin.

He looked over his shoulder and noticed that Faith had tumbled out of the bed. "Sorry. You okay?"

She crawled back over to it without answering.

"Listen to me, Faith, I'm going to be right back," he said, reaching into the glove compartment for the gun. "Just sit still and everything will be fine."

He could hear her crying and it made him even more anxious. "Did you hear me?" he asked angrily.

"Yes," she squeaked.

"Good. Stay in the vehicle."

"Okay."

Ben shoved the gun into the pocket of his hoodie and hopped out of the van.

His cousin, who was now blocking him in the driveway, got out and stormed over to him angrily. "Where is she?" he growled.

"Alex," said Ben. "You really should just mind your own business. This has nothing to do with you."

He balled up his fists. "Answer me. Where is Chloe?"

"Her name is Faith."

"Jesus Christ, Ben! Faith is *dead*. Barbara is *dead*. They were killed in a car accident three years ago! You already know all of this!"

165

Ben shook his head. "No. I told you before – it was staged. Those people were not Faith or Barbara."

Alex laughed coldly. "*Staged?* You seriously think that someone else was driving her car the night she left you?"

"Oh, Barbara definitely had help. She wanted to leave me well before that night and had enough time to plan her escape," he replied, remembering how he'd been called in the middle of the night, unaware that his wife and daughter had even left the house. There'd been an accident and a fire on the interstate. The bodies had been burned to a crisp and unidentifiable. It had been very convenient, so much so that Ben had come to the conclusion that it had been set up. If he believed them to be dead, he'd never go looking for them. But, he was smarter than that.

"For God's sake! The dental records matched, Ben!"

"That's what they wanted everyone to believe. But Barbara's parents had left her enough money that she could have easily bribed the medical examiner and the dentist."

"You're insane! There's no reasoning with you," he replied staring at Ben in disbelief.

"Get back into your truck and drive away," said Ben. "This has nothing to do with you."

"You killed at least one little girl and there is no way I'm going to let you harm Chloe," he said. "Now, where is she? In the van?" Alex stepped around him and began walking toward the back.

Gritting his teeth, Ben took out his gun. "Stop, Alex! Don't make me shoot you!"

Alex froze and then turned around.

"Get away from my vehicle," Ben said, moving toward him slowly with the gun aimed at him.

166

"Don't do this," begged Alex. "It's not too late. You can get help."

"I don't need *help*," he said coldly. "All I need is my daughter and now I have her. Now, get your ass back into your truck and drive away. This is my last warning."

Alex stared at him for a minute and then nodded. "Okay. Fine. I'll leave. I just hope you know what you're doing."

"I do," Ben replied, relaxing slightly.

Alex turned as if he was going to leave, but, instead, charged Ben, knocking him to the ground. They wrestled in the snow, and after a short struggle, Alex was able to get the gun from him. He quickly got to his feet and pointed the gun down toward Ben.

"So, you're going to shoot me now?" Ben said incredulously. "That's it? You never did forgive me, did you?"

Alex laughed coldly. "Forgive you? You mean for having sex with Patty? No, of course I haven't forgiven you. But, this has nothing to do with her. This is about the girl you killed and the one in the van."

"Alex, I swear… I only did it because I knew Patty was a tramp and you couldn't see it with your own eyes. So, I decided to prove what a whore she was so you could divorce the bitch."

Alex clenched his jaw. "Stop."

Ben stood up and brushed the snow off of his jeans. "Hell, *she* was the one who invited me over for coffee and then was all over me."

"I don't want to hear any more about it!" Alex snapped, glaring at him.

"I didn't mean for you to find out it was me with her that day," he continued. "You weren't supposed to come home."

167

"So, you did it all for me," Alex replied dryly.

"Yes! She let me take naked pictures of her. I was going to send them to you anonymously." He took a step toward him. "I told her that it would be for my eyes only, but I wanted you to see what Patty was doing behind your back."

Alex shook his head in disgust. "You really do need help, man."

Ben stared at the contempt on his cousin's face and knew that he was in trouble. Alex would turn him in and he couldn't allow that. He needed a plan and quickly.

"Get back," said Alex, waving the gun.

Ben knew what he had to do.

He imagined the last girl he'd killed and how Barbara had been responsible for it. An innocent girl caught in the middle of a family crisis. Just thinking of the girl's innocence and what he'd been forced to do brought tears to his eyes. He covered his face with his hands. "You're right," he said, making himself cry. "I feel like I'm losing control. I didn't want to hurt anyone. I just miss Faith so much."

Alex relaxed slightly. "I know," he said. "But, she's gone and Chloe isn't her. I have to get her back to her parents. They're worried sick about her."

He nodded slowly. "Yes. You're right. She's in the van." Wiping tears from his cheeks, he began walking toward the back. "I'll help you get her out."

"Stop," ordered Alex. "I'll get her."

Ben froze and looked at him over his shoulder. "Fine."

Alex, still wary, walked around him.

"Maisie, do you want a treat?" said Ben loudly.

The dog started barking in the back of the van. This distracted Alex enough that he looked away and Ben was able to tackle him. They landed in the snow and began to wrestle for the gun. Unfortunately, Alex lost control of the weapon and Ben was able to retrieve it.

Ben scrambled to his feet and aimed the revolver at him.

"Wait," said Alex, raising his hand. "Think about this! You're making a mistake!"

"No, you're the one who made a mistake by coming here," he replied, cocking the gun.

Horrified, Alex tried crawling away.

Ben pulled the trigger.

Chapter 32

CARISSA FOUND JIM'S business card in her SUV and called him.

"Did you know that Ben and Alex were cousins?" she said frantically into the phone.

"Alex? Alex *Richardson*?" he asked, surprised. "You're shitting me."

"Yes! I mean no. I'm not."

"Wow. I guess he never mentioned anything. Are you sure?"

She knew it was so in the pit of her stomach. "I'm fairly certain, although I don't have any proof. By the way, Alex left a little while ago to meet you at Ben's. Is he there?"

"No, he hasn't shown up. And Ben isn't here either. It looks like the place hasn't been used in a while."

"Crap. I was afraid of that," she said, chewing on her lower lip.

"One thing we've learned, however, is that he *was* married and had a child. They died in a car wreck, about three years ago, though."

Carissa's breath caught in her throat. "They're dead? Well, I guess that makes sense."

"What makes sense?"

She was about to tell him that she believed it may have been one of their spirits who'd led her to Castle Danger, but decided to keep it to herself. She didn't want to lose him now that he had some faith in her abilities. Some people were turned off by the mention of spirits and she had a feeling that Jim might be one of them.

"I was just going to ask whether or not the child's name was Faith."

"Yes. You were right about that. And his wife's name was Barbara. By the way, her parents had a cabin not far from here. The Feds just found out that the title is registered under Barbara's maiden name. We're going to check it out."

Carissa knew instinctively that it was where Ben had been staying and wondered if Alex knew about it. She didn't know what was going through the man's head right now, but believed that it had been a shock for him to realize his cousin was a murderer.

"I gotta go. Do me a favor, Carissa, let Paul and Rachel know we haven't given up and are doing everything we can to find their daughter."

"I will," she replied. "What about Alex?"

"If he is cousins with Ben, I hope to hell that Alex didn't know about this all along and kept it to himself. I've known the man for many years. I just can't believe that he'd knowingly let something like this happen."

"To be honest, I don't think he realized it until it was too late," Carissa said, staring ahead into the darkness.

"Let's just hope that it's not too late for Chloe," he replied grimly.

Chapter 33

CARISSA GOT OUT of her SUV and walked to Paul and Rachel's cabin. She knocked on the door and a few seconds later, Paul answered.

"I have some news," she told him.

Looking surprised, he stepped aside. "Come in."

"Hello," she said to Rachel, who was sitting on the sofa and holding a tissue.

Her smile was bitter. "Hi, Carissa. You have news?"

The atmosphere in the cabin was chilly and it had nothing to do with the thermostat needing adjusting. She could tell that Rachel and her husband had been arguing.

"Ben wasn't where they thought he'd be, but Sheriff Collins found an address for his in-laws' cabin, and the police are on their way right now."

"Do you think he has Chloe there?" asked Rachel.

Something told her she wasn't at the cabin anymore, but she didn't have the heart to tell them. "Hopefully."

"So, we just keep waiting. Marvelous," said Paul, sitting down on the other end of the sofa.

"Would you like some coffee?" asked Rachel, getting up.

Carissa suddenly felt compelled to get into her truck and drive. "Actually, I have some things I need to do," she said, her heart beating faster.

Paul looked relieved that she was leaving. "Okay. Thank you for the information," he said, getting back up.

"You're welcome. By the way," she said, looking from Paul to Rachel, "Chloe needs you two to be strong for her. No matter what happened in the past or what happens in the future, do not, for the love of God, fight around her. She's already been through enough and needs your support."

Paul gave Rachel a look that said, 'Can you believe this woman'? "Of course, we know that," he said irritably.

Carissa's eyes bored into Paul's. "You, especially, Mr. Bloom, need to step up and fix what you've broken. You let Chloe down and it's going to take her awhile to trust you again."

He stared at her, his mouth agape.

"What is she talking about?" asked Rachel, frowning. She walked over to her husband. "Paul, you need to talk to me."

"Rachel will find out, Paul," said Carissa, opening the door to let herself out. "You'd better be the one to tell her."

"Sit down," he said, looking defeated. "I'll tell you."

Carissa closed the door behind her, the urgency to get in her SUV and drive almost overwhelming. She raced over to her vehicle, got in, and headed to the place she knew she needed to be. Gooseberry Falls.

Chapter 34

BEN MOVED ALEX'S Jeep out of the way and hopped back into the van. He felt sick inside that he'd shot his cousin, but the man hadn't left him a choice.

Wiping the sweat from his brow, Ben headed away from the cabin, to HWY 61. From there, he turned south. He knew the journey to Alaska would take two to three days and that was *if* he didn't make any pit stops. Having a little girl and a dog with him, however, he knew it would be impossible not to.

Ben glanced behind him and noticed that Faith was sitting up. "Are you okay?"

"I have to go to the bathroom," she said.

He groaned. "Why didn't you do that when we were at the cabin?"

"I did," she replied, looking embarrassed.

Ben remembered that she'd had an accident. Why she needed to go again already was a mystery, but she was a kid and they were unpredictable.

"Let me think," he muttered.

She didn't say anything.

He knew he couldn't bring Faith to a gas station or anywhere that someone might see her. He couldn't go back to the cabin either. The only other choice was the great outdoors.

"Are you sure you can't hold it?" he asked.

"For a little while," she said timidly.

He let out a ragged breath. "Okay. Don't worry, kiddo. We'll find somewhere for you to go," he said, looking back at her.

A look of relief spread across her face. "Thanks."

Ben was still annoyed but he knew that children were like that and couldn't hold it against her. If anything, he needed to try and make her trust him and kindness was all he had right now. Thankfully, he'd taken his pills before they'd left and he was feeling much calmer than earlier.

"I bet Maisie has to go, too. Don't you, girl?" Ben asked, smiling.

Hearing her name, Maisie barked.

"Why don't you give her a treat?" suggested Ben. "There's some in the red canister back there."

"Okay," said Faith.

Ben drove for a few miles and when the sign for Gooseberry Falls State Park appeared, he decided that it would be the best place for her to go. Fortunately, it was shut down for the night and far enough away from the main road to not attract attention. He turned at the exit sign and drove down the winding road that led to the Visitor's Center.

"You'd better put your jacket on," he said, after parking the van and turning off the headlights. "It's cold and the last thing we need is for you to get sick."

"Okay," she said softly.

175

"You're still not scared of me are you, pumpkin?" he asked, watching as she put her jacket on.

Faith didn't answer and knew that she was too frightened to tell him the truth.

Sighing, he got out of the van and walked around to the back to open the door.

"Yes, you're coming out, too, Maisie," he said, grabbing the leash. He hooked it to her collar and then lifted her down into the snow. Next, it was Faith's turn. "Okay, pumpkin, come here."

She crawled over to Ben, watching him warily.

"You're going to have to pee in the snow," he said, picking her up. "The public bathrooms are closed down at night."

Her eyes widened. "Outside?"

He set her down. "Yes. Haven't you ever gone camping?"

"My daddy said he was going to take me next summer," she said.

Ben clenched his jaw. "I'm your father, Faith. Me! Quit talking about that other man. He wasn't your daddy."

She flinched.

Ben took a deep breath and reminded himself that she'd been brainwashed. "Look... just, do what you have to do."

Faith looked around helplessly.

Ben pointed over toward the front of the van. "If you're shy, just go over there and do your business. Don't forget to raise your nightgown up and over your legs, so you don't get it wet."

"What about toilet paper?"

He sighed. Females had to make everything so difficult. "Will napkins work?"

She nodded.

176

"Hold Maisie's leash and stay right here," he said, handing it to her. "I'll get you some."

"Okay."

***

Chloe didn't really have to go to the bathroom. She'd hoped that he was going to take her to a gas station, so she could try and find someone to help her. But, he'd brought her there instead. Fortunately, she'd remembered her daddy saying that Gooseberry Falls wasn't far from their cabin. She just needed to get away from Ben and find help.

Chloe looked toward the Visitor's Center and noticed a light on in the building.

Someone must be there, she thought.

With her heart pounding in her chest, Chloe watched as Ben walked to the front of the van. When he opened the door and leaned inside to look for the napkins, she released Maisie and ran toward the building as fast as she could.

"Faith!" hollered Ben.

Chloe didn't understand why he kept calling her Faith, but she did know that there was something very, very wrong with him and it made her run faster. When she reached the entrance of the center, she found that it was locked and began to cry.

Why had the light been on if nobody was inside?

"Faith!" hollered Ben, running toward her.

Panicking, Chloe decided to try and make a run for it. She turned and raced down the path leading toward the falls.

"Stop right there, young lady!" ordered Ben. He suddenly screamed out in pain and Maisie began to bark.

Surprised, Chloe glanced back to see that he'd slipped and fallen. She watched him get up slowly and could tell that he was in pain. Feeling more confident, she continued running.

Chapter 35

CARISSA WAS JUST pulling into the lot of the state park and noticed that there wasn't patrol car stationed there anymore. What she did see was a white cargo van parked near the Visitor's Center. The back door was open, as was the driver's side door.

Remembering that she'd seen a white van in her visions, she quickly turned off her headlights and made a quick phone call to Jim. Her hands trembled as she waited for him to answer. Unfortunately, she got his voicemail.

"It's Carissa again. I'm at Gooseberry Falls and I think Ben and Chloe are here. There's a van here and it looks very suspicious. Please, get here quickly."

After hanging up, she opened up her purse and took out her pepper-spray. She also grabbed a flashlight from the glove compartment and then quickly got out of the SUV. As she made her way cautiously toward the van, she heard a man scream in pain.

Heart racing, Carissa hurried toward the Visitor's Center just in time to see someone limping down the pathway toward the falls. As she edged closer, Carissa noticed a small Beagle with him. Sensing her, the dog turned around and barked.

Ben snapped his head around. "Who's there?"

She turned on the flashlight and shined it on him. "Where is Chloe?"

"Excuse me?"

She stepped close enough for him to see her.

Recognizing Carissa, a confused expression spread across Ben's face. "What are *you* doing here?"

"Where is Chloe?" she repeated, moving toward his cautiously.

He smiled coolly. "I don't know anyone named Chloe. I'm here with my dog, taking her for a walk."

She snorted. "Right. In the middle of the night?"

"I work a lot and she needs the exercise. Look, I don't know why you're here or who this Chloe person is that you're looking for. Nobody else is out here but us."

Afraid to shine the light away from him, she began calling for Chloe.

Ben pulled out a gun and pointed it at her. "You thought you could fool me, but I see right through you."

Carissa stared at him in confusion. "What? Put the gun down."

"Let me guess, Barbara. You had some cosmetic surgery and decided to skip a few meals?"

She frowned. "Please put the gun down. I'm not Barbara."

"You can't have her back!" Ben snapped. "She's my daughter, too, and you stole her away from me!"

"Look, the police are on their way," she said, staring at the revolver and feeling like an idiot. She should have gotten close enough to spray him with the pepper-spray. "Lower the gun before someone gets hurt."

He glanced toward the parking lot and then back at her. "How did you find us?"

"I guess I was just lucky," she replied.

A cold smile spread across his face. "Well, Barbara, it looks like your luck seems to have run out," he said cocking the gun.

A child's scream echoed through the darkness and then a shrill cry for help.

Ben's face whitened. He lowered the gun and began limping toward the sound of her cries. "Faith?!"

"Help me!" she cried.

Carissa followed him and gasped when she saw Chloe. The child was somehow on the side of the lower falls, clinging to earth and rocks to keep from falling into the treacherous gorge below.

"Hold on!" hollered Ben, shoving the gun into his jacket pocket. "I'm coming for you!"

***

Chloe was frightened beyond belief as she tried to hang on. She'd thought she could cross over the rocks but had slipped. Now her fingers were ice-cold and the rocks were wet, making it hard to hold on to.

"I'm coming," said Ben, climbing down toward her. "Just hang in there."

Her teeth were chattering so much that she couldn't even respond.

"Just, whatever you do, don't let go," Ben said.

A few seconds later, he was pulling her up the rocky cliff and away from the dangerous gorge. Noticing that she was wet and shaking, he set her down, pulled off his winter jacket, and wrapped it around her.

"This is why you shouldn't run from your father when he calls for you," he said, scolding her. "You could have died."

Chloe didn't say anything. She was too busy watching as a woman snuck up behind him from out of the darkness.

"We have to get you back to the van. You're shivering. Are you still cold?" he asked her.

She nodded.

The stranger put a finger to her lips and then motioned for Chloe to move away from him.

Chloe took a couple of steps back.

The woman raised a small can in the air and then whistled softly.

Ben whipped his head around.

Chloe watched as the stranger tried spraying him with whatever was in the can, but nothing came out.

Angry, Ben backhanded the woman and she fell down into the snow.

The woman looked up at her and screamed for Chloe to run.

Crying, she turned and ran.

"Faith, get back here!" hollered Ben.

***

Carissa watched as Ben began limping after Chloe again. Ignoring the pain in her cheek, she got back to her feet, grabbed the flashlight, and took off after them.

"Faith!" yelled Ben.

Coming up behind him, she raised the flashlight and hit Ben in the head as hard as she could.

Unfortunately, it wasn't hard enough.

Ben turned around. "You stupid bitch," he growled, grabbing her by the throat.

Carissa brought her chin down, grabbed the outside of his wrists, twisted then outwardly, and kicked him in the stomach, thankful she'd taken the martial arts classes.

Grunting loudly, Ben let go and stumbled backward.

Moving toward him, she was about to do a roundhouse kick to the face when somewhere along the path, the dog began to bark madly. It was followed by another terrified scream from Chloe.

Her hesitation gave Ben all he needed to slam his fist into her face.

Carissa went down.

Chapter 36

BEN WAS FURIOUS. He'd wanted to shoot Barbara but had forgotten the gun in his winter jacket. Now it sounded as if his daughter was in trouble again and he didn't have time to worry about the stupid bitch. He also knew that if the police were on their way, he needed to grab his daughter and get the hell out of there.

Maisie was barking hysterically and when he reached them, he found out why. A wolf had the two cornered and was growling.

Shocked, Ben clapped his hands loudly and hollered at the top of his lungs, hoping to frighten it away. Thankfully, the wolf took off.

Sighing in relief, he limped over to Faith. Fighting the urge to bend her over his knee and spank the hell out of her, he grabbed her arm. "You *ever* take off on me again and I'll…" he pointed to Maisie, "I'll kill her. It will be your fault, too. Just remember that."

Faith's eyes became wide. "No!"

He leaned down and unzipped the pocket of his jacket. "Then you'd better start behaving, young lady. I'm not playing around. You understand?"

Shaking, she nodded.

Ben looked back to where he'd left Barbara and was tempted to go and search for her. Time was running out, though. He was beginning to doubt that the police were going to show since everything was quiet, but he didn't want to take any chances.

"Let's go," he said, grabbing Faith's hand.

Ben's ankle was throbbing as they took the path back to the van. The pain was so intense that he broke out into a cold sweat, and by the time he reached his vehicle, he was dizzy. He put Maisie and Faith back into the van, closed the door, and was about to get inside himself, when Barbara jumped onto his back. It was too much weight for his swollen ankle to handle and they both went down.

Chapter 37

CARISSA HADN'T PLANNED on jumping on top of Ben, but she'd been frantic to stop him from leaving with Chloe. Howling in pain, he collapsed with her still clinging to him. Unfortunately, within seconds, he had her on her back and was screaming into her face.

"You stupid bitch! I gave you several chances, but you just can't stay away! Now you're going to get what's coming to you, Barbara!"

Terrified, Carissa jabbed her thumbs into his eyes.

Ben screamed in pain.

She shoved her feet against his abdomen and was able to kick away from him. As she got to her feet, she noticed Ben fumbling for his gun and quickly kicked it away. He tried crawling for it, but she was able to grab it first.

"Enough!" she hollered, aiming it at him. "It's over!"

"You are *not* taking my daughter from me again," he growled, getting to his feet.

"Stop right there," she ordered, taking a step back.

Ben noticed her hand trembling and smiled. "You wouldn't shoot me. You don't have it in you."

"To save her, I would."

He took another step toward her and Carissa knew that he wasn't going to back down. Hoping that she was doing the right thing, she lowered the gun.

"See, I didn't think so," he replied, smirking.

Using everything she had, Carissa struck him in the chin with a hard front kick. He landed on his back and didn't move.

Staring down at him in shock, she wasn't sure what to think. She had never actually used the kick in a real life situation, only in training, where everyone wore safety gear.

Gripping the gun, she walked over and nudged him with her boot. Still, he didn't move.

Sighing in relief, Carissa ran to the back of the van and opened it. Right away, the puppy rushed forward in greeting, but Chloe stared at Carissa with big, frightened eyes.

"Chloe. It's okay. Come here," she said, holding her arms out to the girl. "You're safe now."

Still wary, Chloe crawled over to her.

Carissa lifted the child out of the van.

"Where is he?" she asked as Carissa set her down.

"Don't worry. He's unconscious," replied Carissa, grabbing her hand.

"But, where?" asked the little girl, peering around the van.

Carissa looked over to where she'd left Ben.

He was gone.

Terrified, she pulled Chloe closer and pointed the gun toward the front of the van, expecting him to come charging. "Let's get to my truck."

"Okay."

As Carissa and Chloe backed away from the vehicle, they could hear sirens in the distance.

She gave her a reassuring smile. "See, everything is going to be just fine. The cops are on their way."

"But... what if Ben comes back for me?" asked Chloe in a frightened voice.

Carissa scanned the perimeter, wondering where he'd run off to. "I'll shoot him."

Chapter 38

THE POLICE SEARCHED the state park but were unable to locate Ben.

"He really has nowhere to run," said Jim. "We'll get him eventually."

"He was pretty hurt," Carissa said, watching as the FBI agents placed Chloe into their vehicle to bring her back to the resort.

"Good. That will make our job easier." Jim then told her about Alex. "He's alive, but in critical condition."

"Was he conscious?" she asked, horrified.

"Barely. He confirmed that it was Ben who shot him, though, and that they were indeed cousins."

"He had no idea that Ben had Chloe?"

Jim took out a cigarette and lit the end. "No. At least that's what he said."

"He's not lying," she replied softly, feeling it was the truth. Although Alex had made a mistake by confronting Ben on his own, it wasn't to try and cover anything up. He'd only been trying to save Chloe.

"Maybe. Maybe not. Once he's feeling better, we'll question him some more."

"Ben thought that I was Barbara," said Carissa, shaking her head with a grim smile.

"Really? Wow. What a nutcase. I'm surprised he's functioned so well in society. He's gym teacher, for God's sake," said Jim, scowling.

"He obviously knows how to put the charm on when he needs to," said Carissa.

"I just can't believe that his daughter was dead all along and he was searching the countryside for her. There are at least three other cases, with the similar M.O.s, we think he's responsible for. Two of the bodies have been found, including Amy's. There's still one missing."

"He was responsible for all three," she said, no doubt in her mind about it. "Although, I think he blames Barbara for their deaths."

"He tell you that?"

"Not in so many words," she replied. The truth was, Carissa sensed that Ben blamed his wife for every bad thing he'd done, even shooting Alex.

He took a drag of his smoke and blew it out. "If we don't get Ben tonight, I suppose we'd better keep a close eye on Chloe, and her family."

"Yes," she replied, staring off. "He still thinks she's Faith and if he finds a way to get back to her, he will."

Chapter 39

AFTER GIVING A formal, written statement to Jim, Carissa went back to the lodge. Although she was exhausted, she wanted to check in with Chloe and her parents before heading to her own cabin. As expected, the resort was crawling with reporters and cops. It was almost a relief to know that if Ben did try returning for Chloe, he'd never get past the mob.

"Thank you so much," said Rachel, her eyes puffy from crying most of the night. "Chloe told us that it was you who found her."

"I just wish I could have found her sooner," she replied, smiling. It was moments like this that made her appreciate her abilities. No matter how stressful and frightening it could be at times, an end result like this made it all worthwhile.

Paul also thanked Carissa, but had a hard time looking her in the eyes. She knew it was because he was uncomfortably aware that she knew some of his dark, dirty secrets.

"By the way," Rachel said, when they were alone in the kitchen a short time later. "Paul was having an affair. You knew that, though, didn't you?"

"I picked up on it," she said. "I'm sorry."

191

Rachel's eyes filled with tears again. "Me, too. More for Chloe, though. Paul and I have been having issues and I guess I wasn't that surprised either. But it still hurts like hell."

Carissa's eyes searched hers and she knew that Rachel would pull through and meet someone else. She kept it to herself, however. The last thing a woman with a broken heart wanted to hear was that she'd fall in love again. It would just sound… cliché. "I know it's hard, but you're a strong woman and things will get better."

"Right," Rachel said dryly and then let out a ragged sigh. "Chloe is going to be heartbroken when she learns that we're getting a divorce. My parents split up when I was young and it was a horrible experience."

"Are you sure you don't want to try working it out?" asked Carissa.

"Right now, the only thing I want is for Chloe to have some normalcy in her life. But, honestly, I don't think I could ever trust him again. Or Maddy," she said, staring off into space. "Just being near Paul disgusts me. I hate him. I hate her, too."

"You have every right to feel what you're feeling and should definitely take some time to figure things out. Just make sure that Chloe knows you both love her and that you won't keep her from him," she replied. Although Carissa didn't like Paul, she knew that this experience had shaken him to the core and he would now be a much better father to Chloe.

"We'll see," she said. "It was his fault that she was taken. He told me the entire story."

Carissa nodded. "He made some terrible choices. He won't be able to forgive himself for a very long time."

"Good, because I won't either," she said, grabbing some tissues from the counter.

Carissa sensed that the family had a long road ahead of them to recover from the last twenty-four hours. In the end, they'd work through the tragedy as best as they could, but their relationship would never be the same. Nor would their daughter's view of the world.

"Anyway, I just wanted to check and see how Chloe was doing," said Carissa, yawning.

Rachel also yawned. "She's in bed now. You can stop in and wish her goodnight, if you'd like."

Carissa smiled. "I'd like that."

Rachel showed her to Chloe's bedroom. When Carissa walked in, she noticed that the child was still awake.

Carissa sat down on the bed next to her. "Having a hard time sleeping?"

Chloe nodded.

She smiled warmly. "You're safe and sound here. Nobody can get to you now."

Chloe looked toward the bedroom window. "Did they catch him?"

"Not yet, but they will."

"What if he comes back here again?" Chloe asked, turning back to her.

"Don't worry, he won't be able to get anywhere near you and if he shows his face, the cops will arrest him right away," assured Carissa. Even though she wasn't sure of Ben's whereabouts, she didn't feel that he was nearby.

Chloe still didn't look very convinced.

Carissa took her hand. "You know, you were a very brave little girl tonight," she said to her. "You should be very proud of yourself."

"Thanks," Chloe replied shyly. "Carissa?"

"Yes?"

"I heard my Mommy talking about you. She said you had powers."

"Powers?" Carissa chuckled. "I wouldn't call it that. I'm a clairvoyant."

"What's that?"

She tried explaining as best as she could to a child of seven.

"So, if Ben came and took me away, you could find me again?"

Carissa stared down at her, wishing that she could take all of Chloe's fears away. The girl was still terrified and it broke her heart. "He won't, but if he did… I would search the ends of the earth until I found you," she said, meaning it.

Relaxing, Chloe smiled. "Okay."

She smoothed her hair away from her eyes and gave Chloe a kiss on the temple. "I'm going back to my cabin to get some sleep. I'll see you soon, okay?"

Chloe nodded.

Carissa stood up.

"Wait, do you know what happened to Maisie?"

She thought about the puppy. The last time she'd seen the Beagle, Jim had her. "I'm not sure. I think the sheriff may have taken her to the dog pound."

Chloe looked past her, toward her mother, who was now standing in the doorway. "Mommy, Maisie saved me from a wolf. She needs a home now. Can she come and live with us?"

Rachel looked horrified. "The kidnapper's dog? Absolutely not," she said walking into the bedroom.

Paul who'd also been listening in, stepped around the doorway. "I agree with your mother. You'll have a dog someday, but not that lunatic's," he said, looking troubled.

Chloe began to pout. "Maisie wasn't *his* dog. She was a prisoner, like me."

"In a way, she's right," said Carissa. The dog had been used to victimize children when all she really wanted was to love them.

Chloe sat up. "Ben was mean to her. He even hurt her when she was trying to protect me. You need to save Maisie, Daddy!"

Paul and Rachel looked at each other.

Carissa pulled them aside. "I'm not a child psychologist, but something tells me that Chloe and Maisie might be good for each other."

"The dog's going to be a constant reminder to Chloe of what happened tonight," said Rachel, frowning.

"Dog or not, she's never going to forget what happened," said Carissa. "But Chloe will always wonder about the puppy who tried saving her life. She thinks of Maisie as her little champion."

Sighing, Paul walked over to Chloe and sat down on the bed. "I can't make any promises but… tomorrow we'll talk to the sheriff and see if Maisie is adoptable."

Chloe squealed in delight and threw her arms around Paul's neck.

"Score one for Paul," mumbled Rachel.

"If this was a contest, in Chloe's eyes, you're always going to be leading," whispered Carissa. "Paul really doesn't want to do this, but he's making a sacrifice for her. He needs to start putting Chloe first and this is a good start."

"Maybe," she replied with a ragged breath.

***

By the time she made it back to her own cabin, it was close to five a.m. and Carissa was exhausted. She left her mother a voicemail, updating her on the situation and then fell asleep. A few hours later, her mom called Carissa back, excited about the news.

"You should be very proud of yourself. I know I am," she said happily.

"I just wish I could have been out here a week earlier," she said, "and saved the other girl, Amy."

"You're not going to be able to save everyone, honey. Just be grateful that Chloe is still alive and back with her parents."

"I am."

"What about the kidnapper? You didn't say what happened to him."

"They still haven't caught him yet."

"Will they?"

Carissa sighed. "Yes. I just hope they do before he hurts anyone else."

"Let's hope so. Are you coming home today?"

"Not yet. I want to stick around. At least until Chloe and her family leave Castle Danger. It will be a couple more days."

"I understand. I'm just glad that neither of you were hurt. I guess the martial arts classes paid off?"

"Barely. I think I'm going to get a Carry-and-Conceal license," Carissa said. She'd dodged a bullet more than once with Ben. She knew she wouldn't always be that lucky.

"I'm so glad you've changed your mind," replied her mother. "It's good to have, if you're going to be continuing on what you're doing."

"I have to," she replied.

Her mother sighed. "I know. I wish you didn't but... I'm glad that you do. Does that make sense?"

"Totally," she replied. As frightened as she'd been facing Ben, she'd do it all over again to save Chloe. Knowing that he was still out there and searching for Faith, she had a suspicious feeling that they'd meet again. Next time, she'd be better prepared.

Chapter 40

Two Days Later

BEN WAS NEVER found, but the police learned that he'd somehow gotten to the bank and had cleared his savings account of fifteen thousand dollars.

"I know this is probably a long shot but do you have any idea of where he might have gone?" Jim asked Carissa on the phone, later that day.

"No. Chloe mentioned that he'd been planning on taking her to Alaska. But, I don't see him going there right now," she replied. "Not without her."

"Do you think he's going to try and take her again?" he asked.

She remembered the feverish look in Ben's eyes whenever he spoke of the little girl. He truly believed that she was his daughter. "If he finds her, yes. Unless he sees 'Faith' in another girl."

He let out a ragged sigh. "Hopefully, we'll find him first."

"Hopefully."

Carissa had a sinking feeling, however, that Ben wasn't going to be caught anytime soon. She didn't feel as if there was an immediate threat of him going after Chloe again, though, either.

"Speaking of Chloe, I don't know if you knew this but her father adopted Maisie," he said.

"I figured he would," she said, smiling.

"I was a little surprised, considering the circumstances. I don't think I could have done it, if I were her parents."

"Chloe actually thinks of Maisie as *her* dog, and not Ben's. Leaving the Beagle up here, she'd have felt like she'd abandoned the puppy."

"Huh. I guess that makes a little sense. She *is* an adorable dog."

Carissa smiled. "Yes. Heck, I'd have probably adopted her myself if I didn't travel so much."

"I hear ya. By the way, I heard you went to visit Alex earlier today."

"Yes," she replied, thinking back to it. Alex had sworn that he'd known nothing about Ben being a murderer and she'd believed him. Apparently, they hadn't spoken since he'd found him in bed with his ex. "He's still in rough shape."

"He's just lucky that the bullet didn't hit any major organs."

"Right. You're not going to arrest him, are you?"

"For holding back information and taking the law into his own hands? Hell, I should, but... I've known Alex for many years. He admitted that he thought he had a better shot at getting Chloe back by confronting Ben alone. Obviously, he had no idea what his cousin was capable of."

"No, he didn't," agreed Carissa sadly. "And it nearly cost him his life."

"Alex is determined to help us find Ben, when he gets out of the hospital. He feels responsible for him getting away."

"It wasn't his fault," she replied with a sigh. "If it was anyone's, it was mine. I should have never taken my eyes off of Ben."

"Now, don't you go blaming yourself. You got that little girl back to her parents, alive and in one piece. Nobody blames you for Ben getting away."

Nobody but her. It *was* a consolation knowing that Chloe was safe and in the hands of her parents, however.

"Anyway, I gotta run," he said. "They're paging me at the front desk."

"Okay."

Jim thanked her for helping in the investigation and wanted to call her for advice in the future.

"Of course."

"If you get any more premonitions about Ben, make sure you let me know," he said, before hanging up.

"Believe me, you'll be one of the first people I call."

Chapter 41

CHLOE AND HER family left Two Harbors that evening. Before they parted ways, however, Rachel and Carissa exchanged phone numbers, promising to keep in touch.

"Do you think Ben will come looking for her again?" Rachel asked her.

"It's possible. I wish that I could tell you he won't but he's still obsessed," she replied.

She groaned. "I had a feeling you were going to say that. I told Paul that I was getting a gun. Ben tries coming after her again and I'll send him to the other side so that he can reunite with his real daughter," she said angrily.

Carissa smiled. "Speaking of Paul, what's going on with you two?"

"We're still getting a divorce. He wanted to try and work it out but I just can't. All I see is him with Maddy in my head."

"What did he say about her?" she asked, curious.

"The same old excuse people give for having an affair – he didn't mean for it to happen and regrets it." She sighed. "At least he's not in love with her. I think it will be easier for all of us to not have her in our lives. It's bad enough that we're getting a divorce, I just can't imagine if Chloe had to see Maddy with her father."

Carissa sensed that Maddy was heartbroken, though. For her, it had been love.

"Anyway, it's going to be a long ride home."

"I bet." Carissa looked over at Chloe. "Does she know about the divorce yet?"

"No. We're going to wait. She's been through so much and this will be hard on her."

Carissa's heart went out to Chloe. She would definitely be devastated.

"Anyway, I'm changing my last name back to my maiden. Hopefully, that will make it harder for Ben to locate us, if decides to come looking. Hell, maybe I'll even hire a bodyguard," she said. "A cute one that will help me get over Paul."

"You don't want him distracted if he's going to be watching Chloe."

She chuckled. "I'm just kidding anyway. The last thing I need is to start dating right now. Chloe would never understand."

Carissa knew that Rachel wasn't exactly kidding. Paul's betrayal had left her feeling unwanted and unattractive. She decided to share what she'd picked up on earlier. "Don't worry, Rachel. You're going to meet someone eventually who will treat you right and make you very happy. Just don't go looking for him. He's going to find you."

Rachel looked both relieved and sad. "I guess that's kind of relief. Although, I'm finished with men for a while, I think."

She smiled. "Understandable. Just remember, not everyone is like Paul."

Rachel nodded. "What about Chloe? Will she get past this?"

"Chloe will be fine as long as her parents stay strong for her. You can get divorced but try and stay amicable."

Rachel sighed. "I'll do my best."

A squad car drove through the parking lot slowly.

"They're still looking for Ben," she said, as they watched it leave.

Carissa nodded.

"Will they find him?"

"Yes, but I'm afraid that he's going to cause more trouble again before they locate him. Not necessarily with your daughter, either," she replied. Earlier in the day, she'd had a vision of Ben with a woman and a young girl, driving somewhere. They all looked happy and Carissa felt that he'd transferred over his fixation onto the woman's daughter.

"Great," she said dryly.

"To be honest, I think Chloe is going to be safe, but just continue to keep a close eye on her."

"Believe me, we both will," she said.

Rachel thanked her again, and afterward, Chloe gave Carissa a hug.

"Thanks for talking my parents into getting Maisie for me," she said to Carissa.

Carissa gave her an innocent look. "Me? Oh, I didn't talk them into anything. I just explained why I thought it would be good for the both of you," she said to the little girl as Paul put Maisie into the new carrier they'd purchased.

"I just can't wait to bring her home. They said that she can sleep in my room with me."

"I bet Maisie will love that," Carissa replied.

Chloe gave her a serious expression. "She's my guard dog. She'll keep me safe."

"I think she wants to do that more than anything in the world. She obviously loves you."

Chloe smiled. "I love her, too."

"Stay safe, little one," she said, hugging Chloe again.

"You too," said the little girl.

After they left, Carissa went to go check out of her own cabin. After she was finished putting her luggage into the Tahoe, she noticed that someone had left her a voicemail.

It was Dustin.

Her stomach filled with butterflies. Hoping that he was calling for personal reasons, she soon learned that he needed her, but not in the way she wanted.

"Sorry to bother you, Carissa," he said. "I'm working on a case right now and I could really use your help. I know I don't have any right, calling you out of the blue, especially since we haven't spoken in three months. But this involves a missing child and I know you'd want to help if you could. Call me as soon as you can."

As Carissa hung up, she was suddenly hit with the realization that the case he was talking about was a nasty one and involved child trafficking. With a bitter taste in her mouth, she called Dustin back.

"Yes. Of course, I'll help you," she told him.

The End

CPSIA information can be obtained
at www.ICGtesting.com
Printed in the USA
BVHW041403171019
561388BV00009B/626/P

9 781087 808611